The Sentinel
Courage Bay, California
High Winds Strand Hang-Gliding Instructor

An early-morning outing nearly ended in tragedy for Kara Abbott, part-time hang-gliding instructor with Courage Bay's Fly with Frank flight school. Strong winds buffeted Ms. Abbott's glider and sent her off course into a treacherous basin in the foothills of Courage Bay Mountain known as the Embrace. Her glider became tangled in a tree on the steep hillside, leaving her dangling from her wires above a 200-foot drop.

Sergeant Cole Winslow of Courage Bay police department's K-9 patrol and his four-legged partner, a German shepherd named Officer Braveheart, conducted the rescue with the help of parks director Gehlen Lester.

According to Ms. Abbott, one minute she was tangled in the tree branches, the next she was sliding down a cable into Sergeant Winslow's arms. This was the closest call she has had since taking up hang-gliding several years ago. Ms. Abbott works full-time as a music teacher for the city of Courage Bay and is reconsidering her future as a hang-gliding instructor.

Sergeant Winslow suggests that anyone planning to go gliding check weather conditions before setting out. The winds around Courage Bay Mountain are unpredictable and high gusts are not uncommon.

About the Author

CODE RED

MURIEL JENSEN

is the award-winning author of over eighty books that tug at readers' hearts. She has won a Reviewer's Choice Award and a Career Achievement Award from *Romantic Times* magazine, as well as a sales award from Waldenbooks. Muriel is best loved for her books about family, a subject she knows well, as she has three children and eight grandchildren. A native of Massachusetts, Muriel now lives with her husband in Oregon. Muriel met her husband-to-be, Ron, at a photocopier at the *Los Angeles Times.* They live in an old Victorian home on a hill overlooking the Columbia River. Every day Muriel watches freighters, Coast Guard cutters, yachts and fishing boats come and go and speculates about the relationships of those aboard, and those they've left behind. She says it always inspires her.

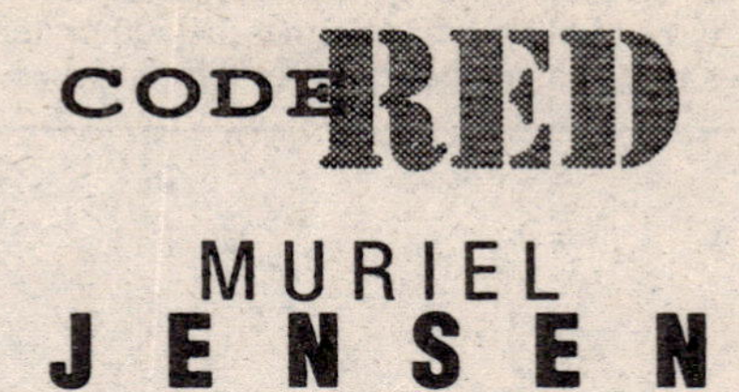

BLOWN AWAY

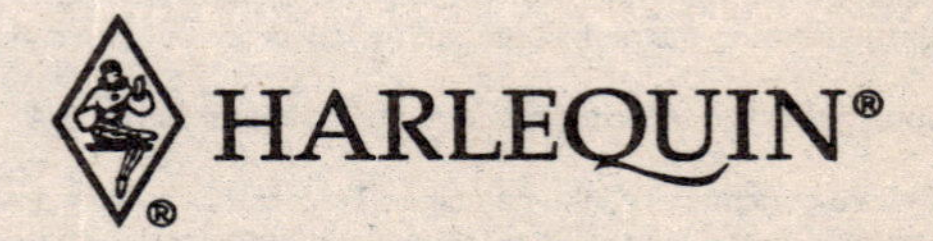

TORONTO • NEW YORK • LONDON
AMSTERDAM • PARIS • SYDNEY • HAMBURG
STOCKHOLM • ATHENS • TOKYO • MILAN • MADRID
PRAGUE • WARSAW • BUDAPEST • AUCKLAND

HARLEQUIN BOOKS
225 Duncan Mill Road, Don Mills,
Ontario, Canada M3B 3K9

ISBN 0-373-61288-5

BLOWN AWAY

Muriel Jensen is acknowledged as the author of this work

This edition published by arrangement with Harlequin Books S.A.

www.eHarlequin.com

Printed in U.S.A.

Dear Reader,

Love makes life worth living, but add a brilliant dog and it's fun as well. I grew up living in apartments and really missed having a pet, except for a brief period when we had a tiny fox terrier. Then I married Ron, who thinks if the dog is bigger than the children you have less discipline problems. We've had a long succession of large and wonderful dogs who've been as dear to us as our two-legged children. Fred, in residence now, is a three-year-old black Labrador that we rescued from the animal shelter. We had him a year when he blew both cruciate ligaments (I didn't know what they were, either, but they're necessary!) in his back legs and has had two surgeries that cost more than our first house. But he's the dearest, sweetest dog. He fetches the paper, protects our cats and holds the sofa down.

But even he isn't as clever as Braveheart, the German shepherd in my book who helps save Kara so that she can fall in love with Cole. I hope you enjoy their Christmas romance.

Good wishes!

Muriel

CHAPTER ONE

OFFICER COLE WINSLOW raced through mid-morning traffic toward the cliffs that hugged the crescent-shaped coastline of Courage Bay, California. Behind him in the SUV's cage, Braveheart of the Castle, aka Mel, a one-hundred-and-four-pound black and tan German shepherd, moved restlessly, his tension palpable.

"Easy, Mel," Cole said, turning inland instead of toward the beach. The panicked call from Fly With Frank had reported a missing hang-gliding instructor. Frank had watched as the woman was blown inland over the ridge by a strong gust and he had been unable to raise her on her cell phone since then. That was twenty minutes ago. With so many of Courage Bay's police officers at the scene of a multiple motor-vehicle accident downtown, Cole and Mel were responding alone.

Mel replied with a low, throaty bark. Cole recognized it as conversation. He and the three-year-old dog had lived and worked together for eighteen months, and so far, Mel was the best partner Cole had ever had.

He was cross-trained for search and rescue as well as simple patrol and narcotics detection.

As Cole followed the road that led into the green foothills, he scanned the trees and brush rising around him, for some sign of the woman. The sail of the glider was yellow and red, according to Frank's description, the woman tall and fit.

"She can take care of herself up there," Frank had said, the fear audible in his voice, "but the wind can slam you into the hillside and splinter you. Find her, Cole. She's got an eight-year-old boy."

Cole heard a vehicle behind him and checked his rearview mirror to see Gehlen Lester's battered Jeep. Gehlen was the city's Parks and Recreation director and a member of the city's High Angle Rescue Team. His hobby was climbing and he'd done it all over the globe. Cole had thanked the fates that he'd been able to locate his friend on a Saturday, when he was usually off on some adventure. Gehlen was the only member of the five-man team Cole had found this morning. He pulled to a stop at the base of a steep slope.

The cliffs before them rose straight up about three hundred feet. Gehlen parked behind him, and Cole leaped out and ran around to the back of his vehicle to open the tailgate for Mel.

The dog flew out as though shot from a cannon, then waited, bristling, for a command.

"Any idea at all where she could be?" Gehlen asked, shouldering a backpack. He was average in height, but wiry and tough. Married three times, he was a favorite with the ladies. At least, those who weren't married to him…

Cole pointed to the highest ridge. "Frank says he saw her disappear over there and go down on a gust. She's probably trapped somewhere in the Embrace."

That fold in the hills had earned the name because the ridge curled in on itself like an embracing arm, creating a concealed paradise of live oaks, big-leaf maples, and madrone. There was a pool on the far side of the Embrace that figured in a Native legend about a woman seeing the man of her dreams reflected in it. Or something like that. But horses were needed to make that climb.

Gehlen frowned worriedly. "Well, let's hope it carried her outside the curl of the ridge. If she went in, she may very well be at the bottom. Nothing for the wind to do in there but slam her around."

"Then we'd better know that before we start." Cole pointed in the direction of the ridge's base. "Mel, find!"

Mel ran off, barking, and Cole and Gehlen hurried in pursuit. The ground was covered with chaparral, a community of fire-adapted shrubs, and the slope was sharp and uneven.

Cole stopped halfway up to drag in air, and used the moment to scan the hillside. The land above them was more thickly wooded, and a bright yellow school bus could be lost among the dark green shadows, he thought fatalistically. What chance did a slender woman have?

Gehlen smacked him on the back as he passed.

"Wuss!" he accused. "I keep telling you to come work out with me instead of sitting in the Bar and Grill, swilling beer."

"I do not swill!" Cole followed him. "I have one, once in a while. You just always happen to come in when I'm there."

"Yeah, yeah."

They were both breathing heavily by the time they reached the entrance to the Embrace. The hills rose almost straight up around them like a wide-mouthed cylinder, the bright blue sky visible at the top.

Cole scanned the green floor of the Embrace and saw nothing.

Gehlen looked up, rotating his body as he scanned the trees and bushes clinging to the hillside.

Cole did the same, lifting his binoculars and turning slowly, carefully.

Suddenly Mel took off at a run, scrambling up the sharp incline, barking in controlled bursts. Cole had come to recognize the sounds as meaning *"I've found something!"*

"What?" Gehlen demanded.

Following the dog's path, Cole moved the binoculars back and forth, occasionally adjusting the lenses to sharpen the image.

If Mel was chasing a wood rat or a skunk, he was in trouble.

But Mel was too much of a pro to do that.

Cole just had to wait and see where he went.

THIS IS A METAPHOR for my life, Kara Abbott thought, dangling limply in the harness she'd set out to test an hour ago. *Hanging by a thread.*

She estimated that it had been about an hour since a gust of wind had turned her effort to check the new harness into every glider's nightmare. She'd been slapped into the side of the hill, where, fortunately, her gear had taken most of the impact. But it now hung uselessly beneath her, its flying and landing wires caught in the same tree from which she hung suspended over a two-hundred-foot drop.

The harness appeared to be uncompromised. She could probably hang here for hours without danger of falling to her death.

But she didn't want to. She had things to do. It was the first weekend in December. She'd promised Taylor they'd go to the Courage Bay Bar and Grill tonight for chili dogs and fries, then drive around town and look at the first Christmas lights.

And she was cold. This was southern California, but the day was overcast and cool. She was also terrified.

To stave off panic, she'd been reminding herself of all she had to do. But her brain kept going back to the question of what kind of tree had eaten her equipment and now held her captive. She couldn't tell from where she was, but she was afraid to wriggle around and look, for fear she'd break the limb she hung from and go hurtling into the chasm.

She was encouraged by all the mature oaks and maples she could see. Thick and sturdy, they could easily bear the weight of a moderate-size woman.

In a flash of near hysteria, she wished she hadn't eaten the chocolate Santa she'd stashed away for Taylor's Christmas stocking. Chocolate went straight to her hips, and what she didn't need at this moment was more weight! But she'd had a rough day at school yesterday, and the serotonin the chocolate provided had lifted her spirits. Teaching twenty-three seventh and eighth graders to take caroling seriously was a challenge.

She hated to think that the issue of whether she lived or died might depend upon 1.3 ounces of chocolate consumed the night before. And the fact that she'd stupidly forgotten her cell phone in the car.

But that had been her life. She'd fallen in love with a smart young man who'd decided several years into their marriage, after the birth of their son, that work was too demanding and he could make a fortune more quickly without the enslavement of a nine-to-five job.

She'd continued to work as a music teacher, trying to honor her promise to him and hold on to the love she'd once believed in, while he pursued every get-rich-quick scheme known to man. When those ended up costing them money rather than making money, he tried selling insurance, selling cars, selling real estate.

Danny finally connected with a dishonest Mill Valley developer who recognized a kindred spirit, and they went to jail together a year ago after a snob-appeal land development turned out to be a swamp deal—literally.

That was the point when the love Kara had tried so hard to save disintegrated completely. She told Taylor that his father had left them to join the military and was serving overseas. Since Taylor was suffering self-esteem issues partly caused by Danny's absence, Kara thought it safest to let him believe his father was still a good person. Or so she'd convinced herself. She knew lying to him wasn't the best idea, but telling him the truth didn't seem like a good option either.

Of course, there was nothing that would put her in a good light as far as her son was concerned. She'd pulled him out of school in San Francisco and dragged him to Southern California, where he didn't know anyone. He was having trouble making friends at his new school, and made it pretty clear that he considered Kara responsible for his father's departure.

She hung limply in the harness, wondering if a fall to her death would be so bad.

Then the wind whooshed down the Embrace, dangling her over the long drop like some weirdly shaped fruit, ripe and ready to fall from the tree. Instantly she stopped feeling sorry for herself and became combative, angrily gripping her harness.

"Fine!" she shrieked at no one in particular. "Fine! Hanging here like a ripe kumquat is still better than any day of my marriage!" And she was quitting this hang-gliding job the minute she got safely down.

At that moment she heard a dog bark—or thought she did. Leaves rustled and her harness squeaked—and then she heard it again—a very distinct bark.

It was dizzying to look down, but she made herself do it, and saw a black smudge moving against the vast sea of green. Two figures raced behind it.

"Hey!" she shouted. "Up here! I'm here!"

The dog barked again, and one of the figures waved something white to acknowledge having heard her.

"Thank you!" she said, raising her eyes to heaven. "Thank you, thank you!"

"THERE!" COLE POINTED to the red and yellow sail barely visible against the green wall of the Embrace. Mel was already halfway there.

"Got it!" Gehlen gestured Cole to follow him. "There's a trail in here. I use it to keep in shape."

Feeling a great sense of relief that they'd spotted her—and judging by her high-pitched shout, she was very much alive—Cole poked fun at Gehlen's superior skills. "Show-off. I'd have climbed the Eiger, too, if my face didn't chap in the snow."

"Again—wuss!" Gehlen returned.

They set off again, the steep slope demanding careful selection of each step and handhold. Calling this a trail, Cole decided, was very generous.

His thigh muscles were screaming by the time they stopped again, about three-quarters of the way to where the woman dangled from the branch of a tree like a Christmas ornament, her glider and its wires hanging all around her. Even Mel seemed to find the going a little rough, and he picked his way over an outcropping to find the meager trail Cole and Gehlen followed.

"Smart dog," Gehlen praised, studying the woman's precarious position. "And thanks for your call, by the way," he added dryly. "I can't believe I left a woman in my bed to help you out."

"That's because you're such a noble soul," Cole replied amiably. "And fate apparently chose to have pity on the woman in your bed."

"Fate never has to do that for you, because there never *is* a woman in your bed. And don't try to pull that grieving widower crap. That was three years ago, and Angela cared more about her career than you, anyway."

Cole turned to his friend a little stiffly. But he couldn't very well condemn Gehlen for speaking the truth, harsh though it was.

"I thought you came to help me locate this woman, not psychoanalyze me," he said.

Gehlen was still staring at the stranded woman, who was having a conversation with Mel. The dog stood on an outcropping about twenty feet below her, barking to tell Cole he'd found her.

"I did," Gehlen said. "But since I don't know how the hell we're going to get her down, I thought I'd work on you a little while I'm thinking about it."

"Hey, puppy!" the woman called down in a voice that sounded both relieved and panicked.

The two men exchanged a grin. Puppy was hardly the term to describe the mature well-trained German shepherd.

"I'll climb up behind and above her," Cole said to Gehlen. "Once I hook her up to me and cut her wires, I'll lower her down to you."

Gehlen shook his head. "I'm the better climber. I'll lower her to you. She's pretty tall. You'll have a better chance of holding on to her until we can swing you back to the trail."

"Swing me back?"

"Yeah. You'll have to hang on the edge of that oak, and I'll send her to you on a line I run between us."

Cole wasn't wild about the sound of that. "Really."

"Yeah."

He was somewhat comforted by the knowledge that Gehlen usually knew what he was doing. And he was probably right about Cole being the one to catch the woman. Long legs in khaki pocket pants dangled from the harness. He couldn't distinguish her features, but he saw a lot of rich brown hair, a red jacket inside the harness, helmet and goggles slung over one arm, and serviceable boots treading air. She probably had a good four inches on Gehlen.

"Okay," Cole said. "I'm sure she'd rather be in my arms than yours, anyway."

Gehlen made a scornful sound and replied quietly, "Yeah. Maybe. As long as you're upright. But the moment you're horizontal..."

"We'd be so up on charges if anyone could hear you."

"What do you want from me? I'm playing cops-and-climbers with you on a Saturday morning, when my plans were—"

"I'll owe you big. Get up there, will you, and help me get her down safely."

Gehlen adjusted his pack and forged ahead. Cole followed, whistling to Mel to let him know he was coming. Mel stood at the very edge of the outcropping, still barking.

"Stay back, puppy!" the woman called nervously. "You're going to fall."

"He's okay," Cole shouted up at her as he reached Mel, who continued to bark excitedly. "He's trained to watch his footing. Are you hurt?"

"No," she replied. "Just stuck. Can you get me out of here?"

"Piece of cake," he replied, as Gehlen began to wrap climbing gear around him and attach him to the thick trunk of an oak that grew almost horizontal, directly under her. "My friend's about to climb up behind and over you. He's going to lower you to me."

"On *what?*" she demanded.

He heard Gehlen chuckle as he scrambled away to put the plan into action.

"I'm not accepting anything less than a staircase with a railing!" she said.

"Didn't bring one of those with us." He appreciated that she still had a sense of humor. "We'll have to do it with a harness and some line." He heard her groan. "Well, that hurts my feelings," he said, testing his knots. "I'm really very good at this."

"Oh yeah?" she said skeptically. "How many times have you done this?"

"Mel and I are search and rescue specialists. We do this all the time."

"Mel?"

"The dog. His formal name is Officer Braveheart, but when I have to shout for him or give him commands, Mel is easier."

"Ah," she said. "For Mel Gibson. Who played Braveheart."

"Very good. You apparently didn't hit your head."

"No. Now, back to getting me down..."

"It's going to be easy," he lied convincingly. "My friend Gehlen is an expert climber. He's going to get into the tree above you, attach another harness to you that's connected to him and cut you free of the wires. Then I'm going to reel you right in."

There was a moment's silence, then she said with wry candor, "I guess I'd be inspired by your confidence if I thought *you* knew what you were doing."

He smiled to himself. As if she had a lot of options but to trust him…

"I thought I introduced myself. I'm Sergeant Cole Winslow, Courage Bay P.D. We're not going to have any trouble getting you down."

"Yeah," she said doubtfully.

Seeing Gehlen climbing out above her, Cole shinned out onto a sturdy limb of the oak. It gave slightly but held.

"What are you doing?" she asked.

"Getting ready to catch you," he replied. "I know you're an instructor at Fly With Frank, but I don't know your name."

"Kara Abbott," she replied. "With a *K*."

As though how she spelled it mattered. But he'd already gathered from their conversation that she was probably a stickler for doing things correctly. She was about to learn, however, that when it came to a rescue mission, each situation was unique. You had to put heart and confidence into it and rely on your training and experience. A little luck never hurt, either.

Still, he had to admit that was small comfort for someone hanging over a two-hundred-foot drop.

"I teach music at Courage Bay Junior High," she added, as he edged farther out on the limb. "The Christmas program is depending on me."

"Nothing to worry about," he assured her. "We'll have you down in an hour."

Another silence.

"Where's your little boy this morning?" he asked, hoping thoughts of her son would encourage her.

"With a friend," she replied. It sounded as though her throat was tightening. "I took the hang-gliding job because he has a long Christmas list involving a computer and trucks with movable parts."

"Trucks. A man after my own heart."

"Cole!" Gehlen shouted from somewhere above her.

Cole looked up and spotted him hanging upside down in the tree from which she dangled. "Yeah!"

"I'm going to hook her up."

"Okay."

Gehlen inched his way down to her and wrapped his harness around her.

"I'm Gehlen Lester," he said in an amiable tone as he worked familiarly at her waist with buckles and harness. "We'll just leave your rigging on and loop mine through it."

"Another cop?" she asked him.

"Better," he replied. "I'm the Courage Bay Parks and Recreation director. Also a veteran climber, so even if you don't trust Cole, you can trust me. There—now you're tied to both of us. When I get back into position, I'll cut your wires and send you down to Cole."

"Oh God. You're sure I can't just wait here until you build a stairway?"

"Sorry."

KARA WAS TERRIFIED. These men wanted to get her down. But as far as she could tell, there was no way to do that without running a great risk of falling. Gliding on the wind was one thing, falling like an anvil quite another.

"We're all connected now, Kara," the cop said with that confident tone.

She didn't trust confidence anymore. Danny had always been so sure of everything, certain the next scheme was going to work…the next investment, the next purchase. But all those great ideas did was get them into deeper trouble.

"You're going to come right down here to me," he added.

"Guys, I don't know…"

"Your little boy's waiting," the cop said.

He'd mentioned her son earlier, but this time terror leaped inside her. "How do you know about him?" she asked, then screamed as the branch she hung from bounced.

"Your boss, Frank, told me," the cop said. "How we doing, Gehlen?"

"Get ready," Gehlen replied. "I'm going to cut."

Oh, dear God! Taylor! What would happen to him if she didn't come home? Would he end up in foster care? Her parents were gone, she had no siblings, no true friendships to speak of; she worked all the time to provide for Taylor and spent what free time she had with him.

"Here we go, Kara!" Gehlen said.

The chaos that thoughts of Taylor created in her mind seemed to extend beyond her. The world spun and dove wildly around her, making her feel panicky and dizzy.

"It's going to work, Kara!" she heard the cop call up to her.

"Are you sure?" she asked desperately.

"I'm sure!"

"Heads up, Cole!" Gehlen shouted, and Kara felt a small tug that set her free. Suddenly she was racing toward death at a speed that made her eyes tear and the wind sing in her ears.

The rich green around her flew by. They'd done something wrong and she was going to plummet to the bottom—she knew it. The thread by which her life had been hanging for years had finally snapped.

She'd known it would happen someday. She'd just hoped Taylor would be working in a law firm by then, or set up in a dental practice, or working for NASA. Oh, Taylor…

Then, before she could prepare for it, she slammed into the waiting arms of Sergeant Winslow.

Terror and the real conviction that this could not possibly end well, that his confidence had been as faulty as Danny's was and they were both going to tumble headlong to their deaths, made her cling to him, eyes tightly shut, teeth gritted, waiting for the inevitable.

It didn't happen.

The harness from which he was suspended swung in a wide arc. She screamed and held on to him with every ounce of energy she had, arms clutching his broad back, one leg curled around his. He held her to him with considerable strength, and she heard the *clink* of a hook as he disconnected her from one rope and tied her to him.

"Are you okay?" he asked.

"Yes," she whispered, eyes still closed, hands still clinging.

"Cole!" she heard Gehlen shout.

"We're fine!" Cole called back. "She's okay. Just a little shaken."

A little? She wanted to laugh out loud.

And when her senses finally overpowered her emotions, she began to be aware of the body to which she clung. It was like a rock, or one of the trees all around them—made from nature's strongest stuff.

And the weirdest thing happened to her: she went soft. Life had been difficult for her for a long time, but the last year had been particularly tough—the move, the expenses involved, Taylor's animosity over his father, and her own pervasive loneliness.

God, it felt good to be held. It didn't matter that there was nothing remotely sexual about it. Her life was now centered on her son and simple survival anyway. But it was wonderful to let someone else be in charge, if only for the time it took to get down to the ground. And this man's shoulders felt as though he could carry her all the way.

She allowed herself one minute, her forehead resting against his shoulder, to fantasize that he belonged to her and she to him. That he was strong enough physically and emotionally to be the man she needed, a man she wouldn't have to support financially. A man who would make Taylor smile. It had been so long.

But reality reared its ugly head as it always did, and they swung wildly in a sudden gust.

She gasped, sure this was it—the end.

"Easy," Cole said quietly, his lips right at her ear. "It's just Gehlen pulling us in. Hold on."

She scarcely needed the encouragement.

"All right! Here we go!" Gehlen's voice sounded much closer, and then a hand caught her arm and pulled. Still she clung to Sergeant Winslow.

"You can put your feet down," Gehlen told her. "You're on solid ground."

Put her feet down? But why weren't they already down if she was on solid ground? Then she realized that both her legs were wrapped around one of Winslow's.

Muscle by muscle, she forced herself to loosen her death grip on him in order to stand.

She really didn't want to. The moment had been so delicious, and something she'd thought she might never experience in her lifetime—someone taking care of her.

Finally her feet met the earth, though she felt very unsteady after dangling in midair so long.

Winslow's hands held on to her arms to steady her, and she peered up into a smiling pair of gray-green eyes in a face that looked just like his body had felt—angular, steady, strong.

It was such a warm and handsome face, and she was so grateful to be alive that strong emotion welled up in her like a healing spring. Certain he wouldn't understand her uttering a heartfelt declaration of love, she did the next best thing. She looped her arms around his neck and kissed him.

CHAPTER TWO

COLE CONSIDERED IT FORTUITOUS that he was still tied to the tree. If he hadn't been, he might have fallen right over the edge of the dropoff when she pressed her lips against his. Well, preferably *after.*

He'd felt a distinctly intimate connection with her the moment their bodies had made contact. Of course, he had helped to save her life. But this was something more, and as she leaned into him, surrendering, he knew that she felt it, too. In a corner of his mind unoccupied with what was happening between them, he became aware of Mel barking excitedly, throwing in the occasional growl in a bid for attention. But Cole ignored him, focusing instead on the woman in his arms.

He didn't entirely understand what had made her kiss him, but figured he didn't really have to. Gratitude in life-or-death situations often took unusual forms. In the last earthquake to hit Courage Bay, an older man he and Mel had found in the rubble of a warehouse had tried to give Cole the keys to his BMW. And a young woman whose child he'd located after he'd wandered into the woods still baked him cookies once a month.

But this kiss was decidedly more intimate, and for some reason he didn't hold back. He returned her kiss, but made no effort to assume control. He felt her fingers in his hair, then his jaw, then fastened on his shoulders while she leaned into him.

When it was over, she took a step back, looking into his eyes. He held on to her arms. Although he was still tied to the tree, it would have terrified her if she'd stumbled over the edge.

She expelled a bumpy little breath and said softly, "Sergeant Winslow…thank you."

Cole was very much aware that he stood on the brink of a precipice—in more ways than one.

"Kara with a *K*, you're welcome."

Gehlen stared at them, his expression half stunned, half disbelieving. "Are you two finished?" With a petulant grin, he added, "I helped, too, you know."

Stepping toward him, Kara smiled and kissed him gently on the cheek. "Thank you, too, Gehlen. Thank you, thank you!"

"You're welcome." He looked from her to Cole, then back again. "Are we ready to go down?"

"Yes," she replied. "Let's go." She glanced at the steep slope, the sheer drop, then back at him with a worried frown. "How?"

"Mel will keep to the trail down the side of the hill," Cole said, as though unaffected by what had just happened, "and we'll follow him. But it's very steep. We'll let Gehlen go first, because he knows what he's doing."

It was a long, slow descent. Gehlen warned of slippery spots, places where there was little protection as the trail followed the edge of the hillside. Mel would run ahead, then double back to make sure they were following.

When handholds were few, Cole stopped to help Kara. He thought she might want to avoid looking at him after that kiss, but she didn't. She seemed almost to be telling him she'd meant it, that she hadn't just been overcome with relief.

He felt momentary alarm, then decided that was foolish. She was very pretty, and it had been a treat to hold her in his arms, to kiss her, but he was a confirmed bachelor and he'd just have to explain that. No woman with a child would want to waste time on a man who intended to remain single.

And she'd feel differently about the whole thing by tomorrow, anyway. Besides, had he and Gehlen switched places as he'd originally suggested, she'd have kissed Gehlen—and would be giving *him* those looks.

After a strenuous forty minutes, they finally reached the bottom of the hill. Cole called his dispatcher while Gehlen got a blanket out of the back of Cole's rig and wrapped it around Kara. Mel sat beside her on the back seat while Gehlen poured her a cup of coffee from Cole's Thermos.

"I'm 10-98," Cole reported when Wanda, the dispatcher, picked up. "No apparent injuries, but we're on our way to the hospital."

"Ten-four. I'll advise Frank and Mrs. Abbott's sitter. And tell her not to worry about her car. Frank says he'll have somebody pick it up and deliver it to her home. Mel okay?"

"Yes. And I'm fine, too, thanks for asking."

"I'm never worried about you, Winslow. We know you're indestructible."

"I might have been injured." He pretended hurt feelings. "It was a big drop. She was caught on a snag way up the Embrace."

"Naw! Maybe if you'd been alone—but Mel and Gehlen were looking out for you."

He made a disgruntled sound.

Then, with studied nonchalance, Wanda asked, "Is Gehlen okay?"

"Yes, he is." Everyone at the station knew she had a thing for Gehlen, who never seemed to notice her because she wasn't sufficiently blond or helpless. A competent brunette who had every detail of dispatch procedure at her fingertips, Wanda had watched Gehlen date every pretty young thing who'd worked for the city in the past five years.

"Want to talk to him?" Cole asked.

"Nope. Lots going on this morning. Let me know when you're 10-8."

"Chicken," he teased.

She cut him off.

Cole went to his SUV, where Gehlen was refilling Kara's coffee cup. She was shaking a little now, he noticed. Gehlen put the Thermos back into the front seat.

"I owe you," Cole said, offering his hand. "With everybody else tied up with the multiple MVA in town, I was desperate. I'm glad you were home."

"Damn right, you owe me," Gehlen agreed, but with a wide smile that said he'd do it again in a minute. "I'm going to think about something really difficult or expensive or dangerous, and you're going to have to come through for me."

"Sure."

"You take care, Kara," Gehlen said, ducking his head into the vehicle to look at her. "Watch those wild winds."

"Thanks again," she said, waving as he headed for his Jeep.

Cole leaned into the back to put a second blanket over her knees. "Getting a little shaky on me, Kara?" he asked gently, thinking her composure looked iffy. She'd been a trouper on the trail, but now her soft brown eyes were brimming with tears.

She sniffed and snuggled into the blanket. Her rich brown hair was disheveled and her cheeks were smudged, but he was struck by just how pretty she was.

"I'm fine," she said, her voice raspy. "I guess I'm just having the classic reaction to the aftermath of a brink-of-death experience. I was thinking about my son."

"The dispatcher called your sitter to let her know you're all right."

Her eyes widened with distress. "Livvie and Taylor knew I was in trouble?"

Cole shrugged. "Not sure. If Livvie's your sitter, then probably. Apparently they've been in touch with the department for the past hour."

She nodded. "Well. If you'll just take me home…"

"We're going to the hospital first. I—"

"But I'm fine," she insisted. "You can see that I'm fine."

"I can, but it's regulations," he explained patiently. "And if you're as fine as you seem to be, it won't take long to check you out."

"I need to see my son," she said firmly.

"I'll take you home the moment the doctor gives you the all-clear. My brother's on today. You'll like him."

Giving her no opportunity to argue, he closed her door, called Mel to him and opened the back so the dog could leap into the cage. Cole ruffled his ears and gave him a treat.

Mel's ears dipped in pleasure as he ate the biscuit.

Cole climbed behind the wheel, turned the vehicle in a wide circle, and drove down the long road to the highway.

In his rearview mirror, he watched Kara Abbott wipe her eyes with a corner of the blanket. Delayed shock was finally taking over.

"Your little boy's fine," he told her gently. "And so

are you. I know that was frightening, but it's over. When you have dinner with your son tonight, it'll be as though this morning's accident never happened."

She scoffed at that possibility and looked back at him in the mirror. "You don't have children, do you."

"No, I don't," he replied, making a point of thinking no further than that. His heart knew the truth.

"You don't forget near misses when you have children. All the ways you've ever wronged them, and even the times when they thought you wronged them but didn't, stay with you forever. And my son is particularly smart and insightful. I guess because he has my undivided attention, he's much more aware of what goes on around him than other kids his age. Unfortunately, that gives him more to worry about."

"It's probably a good thing I don't have kids," he said philosophically, slowing his speed as he reached the outskirts of town. "I'd be feeling guilty continually. And if your son is that smart, he'll just be happy to have you back."

She studied his reflection. "You seem like one of those men who'd be the kind of husband and father most women dream about. Brave, kind, heroic. You're the type that should have children."

"Not true." He knew how wrong she was about that. "My wife almost left me."

She sat up, surprised.

He'd been surprised, too, he remembered, when Angela had told him her intentions.

"Almost?" Kara asked. "She changed her mind?"

"Sort of. She died in an accident in the Rockies before she could follow through."

"I'm sorry," she said quietly. "Where was she going?"

"She was a singer in a rock band. They were doing a twenty-city tour. She called me from Denver to tell me that when she got home, she was packing her things and moving to Seattle. The group had gotten a steady gig there, and living in Courage Bay was holding her back." He could talk casually about that part.

The rest of the story still hurt.

"I'M SORRY," she said again. After a moment, she added, "My ex-husband's in jail. He was sentenced to ten years in prison for real-estate fraud over a year ago. I told Taylor he divorced us and joined the military so he wouldn't wonder why his father never comes to visit."

"Tough thing for both of you."

"Yeah." She sighed and threw the top blanket off. "I was very young, and he sounded smart and laughed a lot, and I liked that. My parents always struggled to make ends meet. Some families pull together and find whatever fun they can in situations like that, but mine just took it out on one another and enjoyed their misery. Danny was like a breath of fresh air to me. He was full of big ideas and I was so tired of my bleak little life."

Kara heard those words lingering in the air between them and wondered why on earth she was sharing all this with a complete stranger. Well. She knew why, but it was crazy. Insane, even.

In that instant when their bodies connected in the middle of the air, two hundred feet above the earth, she'd fallen in love. Or at least in really, really strong like. She knew it might all be based on circumstances, but she doubted it. This man was everything her life needed and had never had, and she felt as drawn to him as if that impact had permanently connected them.

He'd never understand that, of course, so she had to find a way of making a connection that would reach him the way he'd reached her. So she just kept talking.

Telling him about the stupid mistake she'd made with Danny probably wasn't the best way to win him over, she thought absently, but the words just spilled out of her and she didn't seem able to make them stop.

"As you can imagine, life soon taught him that big ideas are nothing without a lot of work to carry them through. Danny just wasn't willing to do the work part. He tried a lot of things, always hoping to find the one that would get him where he wanted to go with a minimum of effort."

Her throat ached a little with the memory of those days and her determination to support him, to help him move on to something else, because she'd loved him, and it was so hard to admit to herself that he wasn't worth it.

"I helped him start again half a dozen times, praying that this time he'd settle in and we'd be happy. But it never happened. We just got deeper in debt, and when he became convinced he couldn't work his way out of it, he went into partnership with a con man and finally got caught. I divorced him and moved here with Taylor a year ago. Taylor had been so upset about his father being gone, and us having to move, that I didn't have the heart to tell him Danny was in jail."

"That's a sad story, Kara," he said with a shake of his head. They reached the hospital and he turned into the parking lot. "Mine's similar in many ways, except that it was my wife's success, rather than her failure, that got in our way."

He pulled into the parking area for the emergency department.

"We're just going to be wasting the doctor's time," Kara said, making no move to climb out when he opened her door.

He offered her his hand. She took it, trying not to let herself make a big deal out of it. It was a nice, large hand, strong and warm, yet gentle as he helped her out of the back.

"Did you say the doctor was your brother?"

"Yeah. Brad. He's a fourth-year resident. He's married to a botanist, and they have a new baby."

"Must be nice to have a sibling."

He grinned as he led her toward the E.R. doors. "It is when they're grown up, but when they're young and pester you all the time..."

"So, he's younger."

"Three years. At least now he's useful—he can fix me up whenever I'm sick."

"Can you fix his parking tickets?"

"'Fraid not."

"Then you're getting the better of the deal."

"Whenever possible."

Brad Winslow resembled his brother, except that his eyes were more gray than green, and he didn't have quite the outdoorsy look Cole had. He was kind, if a little formal, and very thorough. A tie patterned in snowmen was visible at the neck of his lab coat and suggested a sense of humor. Paper snowflakes hung from the ceiling above his head.

"You're in very good health, Ms. Abbott," he said finally, after an hour's examination and another hour waiting for test results. "You don't seem to have any ill effects from being blown off course."

"I told your brother I was fine."

Brad nodded commiseratingly. "He likes to see things for himself. Besides, I think a trip to the hospital is protocol in this kind of situation."

She wanted to ask if Cole was involved with anyone at the moment, but it didn't seem fair to waste his brother's time with a nosy personal question.

"He was very kind to me," she said. "And you'd have to see how he and his friend got me down from the tree to believe it could be done."

Brad laughed lightly as he swabbed alcohol on a

small cut on her arm. "Cole has no fear when it comes to his personal safety. Emotionally, well, that's another matter."

That didn't sound hopeful, though it might be the opening she'd been looking for. "He told me about his wife."

Brad raised an eyebrow as he bandaged the cut. "He did? He doesn't usually share such personal info with anybody, much less a stranger." The bandage applied, Cole's brother studied her speculatively. "But I suppose dangling from a tree together hundreds of feet up in the air makes friends of strangers."

"He caught me," she said, still amazed. "His friend tied us all together somehow, then he cut the wires of my sail and Cole caught me when I slid down the cable. We sort of..." She held her hands apart, then slapped them together, recalling how it had felt when their bodies connected.

She realized she'd been lost in the memory when she heard Brad chuckle. "He's been widowed for three years," he said, "and though there are a few women after him, he's not serious about any one of them."

She couldn't help smiling. "Really."

"Really. The field is yours Ms...."

"Kara. With a *K*."

"Kara."

"Well..." She laughed a little nervously; the situation was odd and made her look opportunistic. "I've only known him about an hour and a half, and I did endanger his life. It seems hardly fair to—"

"You know what?" he said, leaning closer and lowering his voice. "One day when I know you better, I'll tell you what brought my wife and me together. Until then, don't let a little thing like a short acquaintanceship get in your way. If you're interested in my brother, I say fan the flames. That'd be the best thing in the world for him. And judging by your smile when you talk about him, it'd be good for you, too."

"One day when I know *you* better," she said quietly, repeating his words, "I'll explain why that is. Until then, thanks for understanding."

"It's all in the chapter on bedside manner. Get dressed and I'll find Cole so he can take you home." He drew the curtain around the bed and disappeared.

Kara groaned as she reached for her clothes. She wore old things when hang-gliding because they suffered dirt and grass stains and the occasional pulls and snags from brushes with branches. She'd bought her pocket pants years ago when they'd been popular the first time, and she'd worn the old white sweater when she'd painted the floor of the front porch, so it was smeared with dark blue streaks. The red denim jacket had been a bargain-bin purchase she should have left in the car, but it had been a little cooler than she'd anticipated this morning, so she'd worn it. The right elbow was ripped, a button was lost, and it was spattered with mud acquired on the way down the Embrace. If she had hoped to make a favorable impression on Cole Winslow, it wasn't going to happen in these clothes. Of course, when he had first glimpsed her, she'd been hanging in a tree, so what hope did she have of impressing him?

He was waiting just inside the E.R. door when she emerged from the examining room. He waved to get her attention, apparently unaware that some mysterious extra sense helped her zero right in on him.

Cole held the door open for her, then followed her outside. It was now almost one o'clock, and the afternoon was sunny and clear, though the wind was still brisk. Leaves danced, and flags and banners slapped the air.

As they approached Cole's vehicle, Kara saw that Mel waited inside. "Oh no," she said, going to the hatch window to peer in at him. Mel looked back at her brightly and gave one woof of recognition. Or maybe it was admonition. "Has he been stuck inside all this time?"

Cole opened her door. "Please don't feel sorry for him. I walked him around the perimeter of the hospital a couple of times, and he had lunch with three nurses sitting in a van, eating burgers and fries. He got more food than they did."

"That's good." She tapped the window to tell the dog she approved, then got into the vehicle. "He deserves a steak after his work this morning. But, then, so do you."

"All part of the job," he said, climbing in behind the wheel. "Where am I taking you?"

"The old part of town. Orchard Street."

"No kidding." He gave her a smile, then maneuvered carefully around an ambulance and drove out the exit and onto the street. "My aunt lives on Orchard, right across the street from the school."

"Small world. I'm just a block south of the school. My son loves the playground there."

"I'm two blocks up on Sutter. Probably just about even with your house. I'm 673."

"I'm 659," she replied. "You could probably stand on your front porch and see me."

"No front porch," he said. "Mine's a rambling old ranch house built by the architect who created the whole development. So I have a few of the niceties the other homes don't have—a pantry, an office, a metal trellis attached to the garage where you could hang plants or grow vines if you were a gardener. I'm not, unfortunately. But your street was the eastern edge of the avocado orchard that used to be there."

She nodded. "The Realtor said my house is the old farmhouse. Not very fancy, but spacious and two-story, which I really like. I feel more protected being able to sleep upstairs. And there's a big backyard for Taylor. He dreams we're going to put a pool in it someday. He wants to join the swim team when he gets to high school."

"I know the one." He headed away from downtown Courage Bay toward her neighborhood. "I can see a small second-story window from my front yard. And a plum tree or something right by your chimney."

She laughed, inexplicably happy about being within sight of him. She loved her old house, but with no one in it but her and Taylor, it was sometimes very lonely.

"That's my bedroom window!" she exclaimed. When silence ensued, that simple statement suddenly seemed rife with an innuendo she hadn't intended.

"I gave Taylor the bigger front bedroom," she said quickly, needing to fill the quiet, "because his furniture is bigger than mine and he has all these toys that he *never* remembers to put away. I don't do much in my room." Well. That didn't sound good. "I mean, I don't need a desk or a television or anything, because when I finally go to bed, all I want to do is sleep. And I like being able to look up the hill and see all the other houses." She was on a roll here, and didn't know how to stop. "It's hard being new. I mean, a year's still pretty new. I'm making friends, but it's been hard for Taylor."

He cast her a questioning glance, probably wondering what on earth she was chattering on about. But all he said was, "My neighbors have a really nice boy who's also eight. That's Taylor's age, right? Third grade?"

"Yes."

"Blaine goes to St. Patrick's School. We'll have to get them together. Blaine's a bit of a loner because he's smart and has a scientific mind. Sometimes the other kids just don't get him. He likes to visit me and play with Mel."

"I would love that," she said, trying not to sound overeager. She wanted desperately for Taylor to meet other boys his age, but this could be good for *her,* too.

"We'll set it up."

CHAPTER THREE

A TEENAGE GIRL and a young boy ran out of the house as Cole pulled into the driveway of the little white farmhouse. Red geraniums hung in baskets on the porch, and white and pink camellia bushes bloomed in the border that ran along the front of the house.

The boy was dark-haired and husky in long, baggy shorts and a striped shirt. He had hair the same shade of brown as Kara's, though it was cut a lot like Cole's. Taylor probably also had to deal with a cowlick that appeared without warning.

"Mom!" he exclaimed in a voice that reminded the world that he was younger than his size. He ran into her arms. "Are you okay? The dispatcher said you were okay, but then she said they took you to the hospital. Then Mrs. McGinley came over and said she heard on her scanner that you were stuck two hundred feet up in a tree!"

"I'm fine," Kara said, hugging him fiercely. "I guess they always take someone to the hospital after an emergency like that. Are you okay?"

"Yeah," he said. "But I was kinda scared."

"Me, too," she admitted.

She seemed pitifully thrilled that he'd been worried about her.

The baby-sitter, a tall, gawky girl with glasses and a bright red crew-cut, went to wrap her arms around both of them. "Thank goodness you're okay, Mrs. Abbott. We were so worried. I called to ask you if it was all right to take Taylor to a movie, and your boss said you'd been blown away. I called my mom at work, and she called the police and they kept in touch with us."

Kara hugged her back. "Tell you what, Livvie," she said. "I'll pay you double, and we'll call for pizza for lunch before you go home."

"All *right*!" the boy cheered, then noticed Cole standing to one side.

Cole watched the boy's eyes travel over his uniform, then the SUV with its impressive size, polish and gadgets. His expression betrayed awe and envy, then he looked from Cole to his mother and all that disappeared. A belligerent suspicion took over. Classic reaction, Cole guessed, for a kid who loved his father, even though the man was no longer in the picture.

Kara brought the boy to him. "Cole, I'd like you to meet my son, Taylor. Taylor, this is Sergeant Cole Winslow. He and his dog and his friend rescued me from the tree."

Cole held out his hand. The boy looked at it with that same suspicion, but apparently good manners made him take it. There was something touching about that for Cole. Taylor reminded him of himself at that age, even though he'd been skinny and short. Cole's father had left home, too, and he'd been confused about that for a long time, convinced, like most kids in that situation, that he'd done something to cause his father's departure. He'd been mad at everyone, primarily himself, and he'd resisted anyone or anything intended to cheer him up.

At least he'd had Brad to suffer with. They'd fought all the time, but they'd understood each other's anger, and when the other kids made remarks, they could count on each other's support.

Taylor was alone, except for his mother.

"I understand you're a good swimmer," Cole said, wanting to clear away the look of suspicion on the boy's face. He got that from teens all the time, and accepted it as part of the job. Sometimes he managed to change their attitude and sometimes he didn't.

But he didn't want this kid disliking him. He wasn't sure why it was important, but it was.

"No," the boy said flatly.

"He isn't yet," Kara corrected with a speaking look at Taylor. "But he wants to be."

"Have you been to the city pool?" Cole asked, undaunted.

"No," the boy said again.

"I've looked into memberships," Kara explained, "but none of the times that kids can swim work in with my schedule."

Then, apparently aware that Cole needed help, Mel barked once loudly from the cage. The boy turned his attention to Cole's SUV and walked around it to look through the window. A smile transformed his belligerent expression.

"Sergeant Winslow is a K-9 officer," Kara said, joining her son as he peered through the window. "Mel helped him find me."

Cole unlocked the back hatch and let Mel out. "At ease, Mel," he said quietly to let the dog know he was off duty.

As Taylor reached out to pet him, Mel reacted like any other dog happy to take center stage.

"Wow!" Taylor laughed. "Does he go to work with you all the time?"

"No," Cole replied. "I take him with me for special jobs like today, when someone is missing or when we're looking for a perp who's hiding from us."

Taylor turned to Kara and said knowledgeably, "A perp is a criminal."

She nodded. "I see."

Cole bit back a smile. "He's also cross-trained to sniff out drugs. Sometimes when I work nights, I take him in with me. But during the day, he wants to 'help' whether we need him or not."

Mel bumped against Taylor, urging him to play. It had been a long working day for him.

"He's so smart! Can I play with him?"

"Sure."

Taylor ran to the lawn and Mel chased him. In a moment they were rolling around together on the grass, Taylor's laughter loud and enthusiastic.

Cole heard Kara's sigh. "Do you know how long it's been since he's laughed like that?"

"Too long?"

"Much too long." She smiled ruefully. "I'm sorry he was rude. He still thinks his father's coming back, and any man who visits is a threat."

"I understand."

"Not that you'd…that we…"

"I understand," he said again. But she flushed, obviously flustered. He found it fascinating that he'd inspired that kind of reaction. The women he met were either contained and controlled about their feelings, or so free and easy that they had no problem making the first move. Yet Kara was embarrassed about an inadvertent suggestion that she might be interested in him.

Now that he thought about it, that was a curious reaction considering *she'd* kissed *him*.

"Your son will understand, too," he said, with what he hoped was easy grace, "if you explain to him that I'm just a friend. I was married once and have no desire to be married again. Tell him I brought you down from the hill and drove you home as part of my job, so I'm no threat to him at all."

KARA STRUGGLED not to betray her disappointment. *"Well, tell him to get used to seeing me, because I want to come around again"* was what she'd really wanted to hear.

But Cole had made his position clear.

She nodded and said with great dignity, "I'll explain it to him. He's a smart boy."

Cole was watching her face, probably trying to assure himself that she wasn't about to burst into tears or otherwise embarrass both of them by telling him outright that she'd been hoping for something to develop out of their dramatic encounter.

Frankly, she wasn't sure what to do at this point. She needed time to think. She just knew with certainty that a woman who'd had a bad man and then found a good one wasn't going to be easily deterred.

But what if the good man really didn't want to be found? Kara had a feeling that whatever approach she took here would require a delicate strategy.

The radio on Cole's lapel crackled and he answered it.

"Are you 10-8?" a woman's voice asked.

"I've just dropped Mrs. Abbott at home," he replied. "I'll be there in about five minutes."

"Ten-four."

Kara turned to her son and the frolicking dog. "Taylor, Sergeant Winslow has to get back to work."

Taylor, trapped under Mel, was giggling uproariously as the dog licked his face. Kara tried to break them up, but a laughing Taylor rolled toward her, away from Mel, and dragged her down with him. The dog slurped her several times before Cole whistled sharply.

Mel went to his side and sat. Cole told him to stay and came to offer Kara, then Taylor a hand up.

"You're so lucky!" Taylor said to Cole, her son's earlier animosity dispelled by Mel's good nature. "What a great dog. And what a great truck!"

"He is a great dog," Cole said. Mel was at attention now and not responding to Taylor, though the boy stroked his head. "I live just a couple of blocks up the hill. If you want to come by once in a while and help him get some exercise, that'd be good. He gets bored on my days off and when he's not on duty."

Kara was surprised that he'd extended the offer, considering his insistence that he was a happy bachelor. It had to be clear to him that involvement in her son's life was going to involve him in hers to some degree.

Taylor looked eager, then suspicious again.

"My neighbors have a son your age who likes to hang out at my place," Cole told him. "I bet you'd like him."

"Nobody likes me," Taylor said with a candor that tore at Kara's heart. "I don't like a lot of stuff other kids like. And I'm bigger than them."

Cole nodded. "Blaine likes to build things and mess around with his trucks. I did, too, when I was your age. And don't worry about being bigger than the other kids. When you get older, girls like that, even if other guys don't."

That look again—eagerness followed by suspicion.

"Up to you," Cole said. "Your mom knows where I live."

"You want to be her boyfriend, don't you?" Taylor asked, following Cole as he opened the back of the vehicle for Mel to jump in.

Cole shook his head with a dispiriting lack of interest, Kara thought. "No. But your mom's a very nice, very brave lady, and since I live nearby, I thought we could be good neighbors. That's all."

Taylor leaned against the side of the truck as Cole reached inside and readjusted the blanket Mel lay on. "That's 'cause you know she's a good baker, right? Mrs. McGinley's our neighbor and she's always coming over for coffee cake."

That got Cole's attention. He turned to Kara with an interested smile. "You're a baker?"

She didn't waste time being modest, but blew on the fingernails of her right hand and buffed them against the front of her jacket. "I am." She held her fingers away from her and studied the shine. "Coffee cakes, quick breads, mostly. But I can do other things."

"Tell me more," Cole said.

Before Kara could reply, Taylor jumped in with the enthusiasm of a pitchman. "Her orange-cranberry ring is a killer! It won a blue ribbon at the county fair back home three times in a row. And she makes really great almond-butter Danishes."

"Really." Cole closed the hatch. "Well, Taylor, if you do come to exercise Mel, maybe you could bring a piece of this orange-cranberry ring with you."

Not your mother, Kara noted, *just her coffee cake.*

The sound of the telephone carried through the open front door. Livvie ran to answer it. Kara wanted to thank Cole for what he'd done this morning. With Taylor all ears, she chose her words carefully.

"Thank you so much for coming to my rescue," she said, holding out her hand. As she spoke the words, it occurred to her that they were true on several levels, even if Cole didn't see that yet. For the first time in a long time she had new hope. "I know how dangerous that was for you, and I appreciate the courage required to risk yourself for someone else's safety. I'm very grateful."

He shook her hand. She remembered that strong and warm touch.

"All in a day's work," he said with a smile, his eyes lingering for a moment on her mouth.

Yes! He wasn't as disengaged as he'd have her believe.

He offered his hand to Taylor, who took it with reluctance. "I have Monday, Tuesday and Wednesday off this week," Cole said. "You're welcome to come over after school anytime. Just make sure you check with your mom—and call first. I'm working on the house, so I'm usually home." He climbed into the rescue unit, and Kara drew Taylor out of the way as Cole turned and headed down the driveway with a tap of his horn.

"You like him?" Taylor asked her as they walked toward the front door. Her son was a little more remote now than he'd been when she'd first come home.

"He saved my life," Kara replied. "It's hard *not* to like him. And he was very nice to you, even though you weren't very friendly to him at first."

"Well," he said defensively, "what if you get a boyfriend and Dad comes back?"

"Honey, I'd just like to be friends with Sergeant Winslow, but I've explained over and over that Dad isn't coming back. He's got a job with the military over in Europe and he's going to stay there. He told you that when he left, remember? He said he wouldn't be back." There it was again—the comforting lie that tripped off her tongue so easily. She had to find a way to tell him the truth, but not while he was worried about so many other things.

"Being friends is how sex gets going," Taylor said.

Kara stopped at the foot of the porch steps, nonplussed. "What!"

"I know all about it," her son replied confidently. "Finlay Kirk's mother said she was just friends with Mr. Kirk when they worked together in the same law firm. Then they fell in love. When you fall in love you have sex. That's the way it goes. She didn't tell me that part—I just figured it out."

Finlay Kirk lived across the street and was one of the few children in the neighborhood that Taylor could relate to. She'd skipped a grade, and though she was mature for her age, all her classmates considered it uncool to keep company with her because she was a year younger. Taylor often met her at the playground, and Kara was happy to see that he appreciated her.

"While that might be true in a lot of cases..." Kara said, urging Taylor up the steps. Not sure why she was telling him this, she said, "Sergeant Winslow was married and his wife died."

"And he misses her?"

"I'm sure he does. I really don't think he wants to get married again."

Taylor sighed. "Well, that's not good."

"Why not? I said he *doesn't* want to get married. I thought you'd be happy about that."

He gave her a disgruntled look. "But you always figure out how to get people to do things. There's lots of stuff I never want to do, and you always explain it to me and I end up doing it anyway—even when I *really* don't want to. So even if he thinks he doesn't want to get married, I bet you'll change his mind."

Kara hugged her son to her, suddenly feeling better about everything.

"NOW, WHY wouldn't you want to get to know a beautiful woman like that?" Brad asked Cole. They sat at their aunt Shirley's table, spooning up a rich ham, potato and vegetable casserole and catching up on what had happened in their lives over the past week. Brad's wife Emily usually joined them, but she was at a baby shower tonight.

Shirley Bowers was Cole and Brad's maternal aunt. She'd moved to Courage Bay four months ago, after the death of her husband.

"I've already learned a lot about her," Cole said, passing Brad a basket of rolls. "That hour and a half on the Embrace was pretty distilled."

"He didn't say he didn't *want* to get to know her," Shirley corrected, finally sitting down at the head of her stately mahogany table. It took up most of the space in the tiny dining room, but Shirley had refused to part with it. An antique that had been in the family for years, the table had been moved from her three-story house in Portland, Oregon, to her cozy but modest little place in Courage Bay. "He said, 'I don't intend to have a relationship with her.' That's code for, 'I don't want her to get to know me.'"

Cole sighed. His aunt had moved closer to him and Brad to bring a sense of family into their lives, and she certainly had. She'd instituted Sunday night dinner at her home, and nothing he or Brad did ever went without comment or a few words of advice.

Brad laughed smugly. "Aunt Shirley's got your number, Cole. And if you ask me, I think that Kara Abbott would *like* to have it. She looked at you like you were some kind of hero."

"I was." Cole struck a heroic pose. "You should have been there."

"I've seen you in action." Brad pointed to the butter dish with his knife and Cole passed it to him. "So, show some guts where she's concerned. Break free of the spectre of Angela. That wasn't your fault. You gave up a lot for her, and she wouldn't give up anything for you."

Cole agreed. That was pretty much the way it had been in his marriage. "The thing is, if it's not about doing what you think your partner needs, what is it about?"

Brad buttered his roll, then put both roll and knife down, his expression serious. "Right now, it's about the incredible love that I feel for Emily and our beautiful baby. I almost can't see beyond that to analyze it. And I know it's the same for Emily."

Cole was sincerely happy to hear that. "Then go with it. Love is a wonderful thing. I thought I had it once and then it was gone. But I'd like to figure out why, before I try again." Wanting to divert the conversation from his own predicament, he studied his brother for a moment. "You know, you're looking pretty good for someone who's probably not getting much sleep."

Brad rolled his eyes. "Fortunately, my job is the best training there is for sleep deprivation. Residents live on coffee and the hope of forty winks somewhere quiet."

"How's Emily coping?"

"She loves that baby so much she could probably do without sleep—and me."

The teasing note in Brad's voice told Cole his brother wasn't serious.

"But you were essential to the production of the baby in the first place. I'm sure Emily realizes this and will want to keep you around." Cole let his words of encouragement sink in, then said with weary resignation, "I personally see little value in your role here on Earth, but I'm sure your wife does."

Brad leaned across the table with a frown. "Nice talk. Who set your broken arm not so long ago and drove you to the E.R. *on his day off*?" The last words were spoken with an air of injured dignity.

Cole leaned toward his brother. Brad was referring to a mishap in an E.R. versus police department football game. "Who tackled me at the base of that maple tree with the big root sticking up and caused that arm to be broken? *On the first day* I'd *had off in thirteen days?*"

Brad was trying hard not to smile. "You were the opponent. I was supposed to stop you from scoring."

"Well, you did."

"Didn't stop you from scoring with the babes, though. Every woman in your department and every woman in mine went to visit you."

Cole shrugged with false modesty. "I got the charm, you got the annoying personality."

"If this doesn't stop," Shirley threatened, "there's no dessert. And I know how you boys are about chocolate cake with sour cream frosting. You both have enough of my lovely sister in you to charm anyone, and enough of your no-good father to counteract it, so you're going to have to create your own powers of persuasion. Both of you!"

They subsided, but when she went into the kitchen to get the coffeepot, Cole leaned toward Brad and said under his breath, "If we lose out on dessert, it's all your fault."

"Is not!"

"Is, too!"

KARA STOOD IN FRONT of the seventeen students who made up her carol chorus and waved her hands to capture their attention. Some were talented, some were simply enthusiastic, but all were infected with the excitement of the season even though it was only early December.

They were rehearsing in preparation for caroling at several nursing homes and the hospital, and were even offering their services for paying gigs at office parties and similar events. The money they made would go toward a trip to a choral competition in Seattle in the spring. The kids were thrilled about the project, and Kara found it a constant struggle to keep them on track.

She was just running through some rather challenging harmony in "Good King Wenceslas," when Loren Ford, Courage Bay Junior High's principal, wandered into the music room. Kara gave her students the signal to stop.

"Good afternoon, ladies and gentlemen," Loren said. He was a tall, nice-looking man with the good-humored firmness essential in dealing with budding teenagers. The students liked him and he seemed to like them. "You sounded so good from my office that I had to come see for myself. How's it going?"

The choir responded as one, their replies unintelligible. Then Jared Watson, the self-appointed spokesperson, raised his hand from the middle of the group. He was an eighth grader. "It's going well, Mr. Ford. When people hear us downtown, we're going to get more gigs than the Rolling Stones."

"I'm sure you're right, Jared," the principal said.

Kara knew that Loren was acquainted with this student because of the many times the boy had been sent to his office. Jared was tall, gangly and smarter than his marks indicated. He also loved to stir things up for the simple pleasure of seeing what developed. It was Kara's belief that one day he was going to become a revered statesman, or a hitman for the mob. She couldn't decide which.

"Thanks to Mrs. Abbott!" Amy Carmello said. She was the group's emotional cheerleader, a small, plump blonde who alerted everybody whenever a member of the group was sick or just blue and in need of support.

At her words, the kids applauded.

"Let me hear that last chorus again while I have a quick word with Mrs. Abbott about the school program," Loren instructed.

"Okay." Kara nodded at the choir. There was a lot of throat-clearing and fidgeting before they could begin. But once they came through with the first couple of bars, Kara followed the principal to the classroom doorway.

"Kara," he said, hands in his pockets as he looked down at her, a serious expression on his face. "What do I have to do to get you to go out with me?"

"Loren." Kara glanced toward the students and saw that Patty Kramer, who would probably be on Broadway one day, was conducting the group through one of their jazzier tunes. "You shouldn't even bring this up during—"

"I know," he interrupted. "It's inappropriate behavior, but you leave me no other choice. You don't return my calls to your home, and when I try to catch you after school, you always have a doctor's appointment or some other excuse to avoid me."

"That's because I've made it clear more than once that I have no interest in dating," she said quietly. "My son and my work are all I have time for." When he looked disappointed, she added reasonably, "Loren, you're a very nice man. Don't waste your time on me."

He sighed. "I don't consider it wasted. Kara, come to the city Christmas Ball with me. If you have a miserable time, I promise I'll get the message. You're going to have to be there anyway to direct the choir."

That was true. The carol chorus had been invited to sing three numbers at the ball during the band's break—and they were being paid. They were thrilled at the prospect.

But she didn't want to go with Loren. He was kind and fun to talk to, and she respected his work as principal, but she felt no spark of romantic interest. How different, she thought, from the way she felt about Cole Winslow. She'd met him only once, but the spark she'd felt had been only too real. Of course, the situation might have been responsible for that, but not completely.

She smiled at Loren. "I'll be there," she said. "Maybe we can have a dance."

"Kara..."

"If you keep this up," Kara warned softly, "the kids are going to suspect something. Jared's watching us already."

He looked up and saw that she was right. While the others sang on, following Patty's direction, Jared watched Kara and Loren.

"It's Christmas," Loren grumbled. "I know you have your son, but the season calls for love and romance, kissing under the mistletoe and sleigh rides...."

She laughed softly. "This is Southern California."

"I was going to take you to the mountains, to Big Bear Lake."

"I appreciate the thought, Loren. But I'm really not interested."

At that moment, Carrie Wolf walked by the door. Carrie was the girls' track coach and the health teacher.

Kara could tell she was interested in Loren, but he didn't seem to notice her.

Kara almost laughed out loud. In this junior high, it seemed to be the staff's hormones that were running wild, not the kids'.

"Look, Loren," she said. "I really have to get back to my class."

He conceded her point with a reluctant nod, then waved in the direction of the students. "Keep it up!" he shouted over their voices. "I'm very proud of you." To Kara, he added under his breath, "You know where to find me when you change your mind."

"I do," she assured him, closing the door behind him. She hoped this situation with Loren wasn't going to become awkward.

Jared smirked as she took her spot at the podium, but she ignored him and turned to whisper thanks to Patty. The choir was coming to the end of "Santa Baby," and Kara directed them to a lively finish.

"Excellent," she praised as the last note died away. "You're going to make a fortune for our trip." The students began to chatter as they packed up for their next class. "But before you go," Kara said, raising her voice to be heard, "we have to talk about our gift-wrapping venture at the downtown mall." It was another fund-raising project they'd taken on to make more money.

"We're starting next weekend, and we have a few blanks in the sign-up sheet. I know Sunday is a family day, but if anyone can fit in even an hour, it would help a lot. I can pick you up and take you home—just let me know if you need a ride. I'll bring cookies to munch on if you'll all buy or bring your own drinks to keep you going."

"I'm bringing a six-pack," Jared said. Everyone laughed.

"A six-pack of cola would be fine," Kara replied without giving him the horrified reaction he was hoping for. "I have everything else we need. Maggie, is your mom still willing to let us use her table?"

Maggie Hutton, small and dark and the backbone of the girls' basketball team, nodded. Her mother was a caterer and had offered to lend them a banquet-length table to work on. Kara had bought two bulk rolls of wrap—one suited for adults and one for children—and the stationery store had thrown in bows and gift tags.

"Great! Please thank her for us. Who's in charge of thank-you notes to supporters?"

Amy raised her hand. "Mrs. Hutton is already on my list."

Kara should have known. She should be as organized as Amy.

"Everyone remember to wear school colors when you show up to help. We'll be at the mall every weekend between now and the end of school, and once Christmas vacation starts, we'll be there every afternoon and evening. I'm counting on everyone to help, okay?"

Kara might have wished for a more enthusiastic response.

"Master list is on the board if anyone wants to add their name to it." Several students complied. "If you want to work with a friend, that's fine," Kara reminded them. "Just make sure your behavior is professional at all times. No rough language or shrieky laughter. Remember, you're representing the school."

The bell rang and the students streamed toward the door, some pausing to shout or wave goodbye. Kara waved back, admonishing them to be careful—Santa was watching, and their Christmas-morning bounty depended upon their good behavior.

That brought loud groans, followed by laughter, as her students hurried off. They were noisy and troublesome...and she loved every single one.

As she was packing up her briefcase, her cell phone rang. She dug it out and felt a moment of alarm when the caller ID showed a number at Courage Bay Hospital.

Taylor! Something had happened to Taylor!

"Hello?"

"Hi, Kara, it's Cole," a deep male voice answered.

Focused as she was on Taylor, she couldn't imagine why Cole Winslow was calling her.

"Cole Winslow," he repeated after a moment. "You remember. Eagle of the Embrace?"

"Eagle of the...?"

"Okay, flying squirrel," he corrected.

Unable to form a coherent thought, she ignored his teasing and asked anxiously, "What's the matter? Has something happened to Taylor?"

"No," he replied quickly. "Why would you think that?"

"Because you're calling me from the hospital. My caller ID—"

"No, no. I'm sorry if I frightened you—"

His deep voice sounded sincerely apologetic—and warm. Now that she knew nothing was wrong with her son, that pall of fear left her and she was able to focus on the rich sound.

"I'm calling from the hospital because I followed an MVA that I had to talk to. And now my shift's over. I have a little paperwork to do at the station, then I'm heading home."

"Oh." She couldn't think of anything more intelligent to say. Cole Winslow had finished his shift and had called *her.*

Her momentary exhilaration was dashed when he said, "I wondered if Taylor wanted to come over and play with Mel."

She was torn between the knowledge that her son would probably be thrilled, and the realization that she'd been conspicuously left out of the invitation.

"And," he added suddenly, "if you wanted to bring some coffee cake, I'll make coffee."

Yes! "How did you get my cell phone number?" she asked.

"From the initial call on you the day you blew off course. Frank had been trying to reach you on your cell but got no response. He gave the number to the dispatcher, who gave it to me."

"Oh." And he'd *saved* it. She shook her head to clear it, thinking she was going to have to do better than "Oh."

"Want to come?" he prodded.

"Uh...yes. I'm sure Taylor will want to, but I don't pick him up for another half hour."

"Fine. So—forty-five minutes?"

"Okay."

"It's 673 Sutter."

"Got it." *She'd* saved his address.

CHAPTER FOUR

OKAY, WHAT HAD HE DONE? He'd intended to invite Taylor and then he'd heard the high, slightly breathy sound of her voice and been transported back to that moment on the Embrace when she'd kissed him. Suddenly he wanted to see her again.

No, that wasn't exactly right. He *had* to see her again. Her voice had played over in his brain for the past few days. He'd remembered odd things about her—the little gold sunburst in her irises. The small scar under her right eyebrow. And, much to his consternation, the way it had felt after she'd slammed into him on Gehlen's contraption. She'd settled into him—her breasts against his chest, the cradle of her hips against him, the curl of her leg around his—just the right fit.

What had he been *thinking?* he wondered now as he drove back to the station.

Calling Kara had seemed reasonable this morning. He'd thought a lot about her son since last Saturday. Taylor sure reminded Cole of himself at that age, fatherless and with a chip on his shoulder. And Taylor was new in town and having difficulty making friends—a guaranteed recipe for loneliness.

He could help Taylor, Cole thought. The little boy had clearly taken to Mel, and though he didn't seem to think much of Cole, that could probably be rectified. Cole had a big backyard, a rec room with a pool table, a plasma TV, and enough action films to stock a theater. He and his friends from the department liked to watch police procedural films both to criticize and to learn from them. The methods of investigation in the movies were often faulty, if not downright illegal, but they always provided fodder for great discussions afterward.

He'd intended to call Kara simply to invite her son over. Then his brain had malfunctioned, and he'd heard himself invite her, too. But that was only reasonable—she'd want to make sure Taylor was in safe hands. He just hoped it hadn't sounded too much like an afterthought.

He hurried through his paperwork, changed his clothes, then rushed home to straighten up and put on a pot of coffee. Mel followed him from room to room, aware that something was going on. When the doorbell rang he barked excitedly and ran ahead of Cole to greet the visitors.

Cole pulled the door open and felt a twanging sensation in the region of his chest. A plucking of his heartstrings? Good Lord! The notion was sappy and completely absurd. So what if she was pretty and he hadn't had any action in a long time. Well, actually, he'd had a fair amount of it, but it hadn't been very satisfying. In fact, he'd begun to wonder if the whole process was losing its luster.

And yet he felt decidedly turned on simply looking at this woman.

She wore gray slacks and a red turtleneck, and a necklace of silver reindeer with silly expressions. Just above the rounded curve of her breasts rested a silver Rudolph with a blinking red nose.

Her reddish-brown hair was caught up in a loose knot, and wispy bangs skimmed the tops of her eyebrows. An oddly shaped dark brown leather bag hung over her shoulder, and in one hand she held a plate covered in foil. Her other arm rested on Taylor's shoulder.

Taylor sank to his knees in front of Mel, who stood beside Cole, thick tail beating the air as he licked the boy's face.

"Hi," Kara said, smiling into Cole's eyes. She leaned down to her son. "Taylor, if there's a person and an animal in the same room, it's customary to greet the person first. Particularly if you're a guest in his home."

Taylor scrambled to his feet. "Sorry. He's just such a cool dog."

Cole dismissed the need for an apology with a shake of his head. "It's okay. I think of him as another person. And I like him better than a lot of people I know." He pointed toward the back of the house to French doors that led outside. "You can go into the backyard if you want. There's a big red rubber bone out there that he loves to catch."

"Okay. Come on, Mel!" Taylor ran through the house and Mel followed, barking in anticipation.

"Unless you want to have milk and coffee cake..." Cole shouted after him.

He stopped at the opened doors. "I can have that anytime! I'd rather play with Mel!"

Cole waved him outside, then ushered Kara in.

KARA LOOKED AROUND as she followed Cole through a large, rustic living room. The furniture was an eclectic mix—an overstuffed blue and gray sofa and chairs, large oak coffee table almost nautical in style, contemporary bookcases and entertainment unit, and wicker stools pulled up to a bar that separated the kitchen from the dining area.

Cole's home was comfortable-looking and smelled vaguely of citrus and Cole's musky aftershave.

The kitchen was large and open, the white countertops so clean that she'd wager he seldom cooked for himself. Dark blue curtains hung at the windows, and hardwood floors stretched from the kitchen through the living room.

"You must have a housekeeper," she said, placing the coffee cake on the counter. "This is so much tidier than my kitchen."

He grinned as he reached into an overhead cupboard for plates. "I'm not feeding an eight-year-old boy, but yes, I do have a housekeeper. She comes once a week. Fortunately, that was yesterday, otherwise you wouldn't be impressed. Cream and sugar in your coffee?"

"Do you have artificial sweetener?"

He winced. "No. Sorry."

"That's okay. Just a little cream."

"Two-percent milk?"

"Perfect."

As he dug into a drawer for a knife, she noticed a stack of boxes in one corner of the kitchen, a giant teddy bear sitting atop like a very cheerful Buddha.

"What's all this?" she asked, heading over to have a look. As she got closer, she saw what the boxes contained—a Ping-Pong set, several DVDs, a Trivial Pursuit game, a chess set, tools. Bags from department stores were propped up around the boxes, and a framed print leaned against the front of the pile. Skis were propped behind.

"Christmas shopping," he said, coming to join her. "I'm almost finished. My aunt's a problem. My brother and I want to go in on something together, but he's been pretty busy and we haven't had a chance to talk about it."

She nodded, unable to resist reaching for the bear. "May I?"

"Sure."

She took the giant bear into her arms. It was half her height and wonderfully soft. "Is this for the baby?"

"Right. You think it's too big?"

"Oh, no. Teddy bears can't be too big. Taylor has one like this, and when he was little, he used to sit in its lap and talk to it. I think he liked it more than he did me some of the time." She put the bear back on its perch and studied the other purchases. "Are the skis for your brother?"

"Yes. His wife's a good skier, so he's learning. And there's a down jacket in my closet."

She turned to him, amazed and charmed at the same time. "I've never known a fun-loving guy to do his Christmas shopping early."

"Fun-loving guy?"

She shrugged. "You know what I mean. Stuffy, organized types tend to shop early, but I used to clerk part-time in a lingerie store, and I swear, most men came in on Christmas Eve."

He folded his arms, looking serious. "You've probably made some sort of demographic analysis there. It does stand to reason that 'fun-loving men' would shop in a lingerie store. What was the hottest selling item?"

Although he kept a straight face, Kara was sure he was teasing her. "Teddies," she replied.

He looked puzzled, then glanced up at the bear.

"Not that kind," she laughed. "The bra and panty one-piece. Black lace teddies paid the store's rent."

"Ah. And do you own one?"

Why should that fluster her, when it was probably just payback for calling him a fun-loving guy? But her cheeks grew warm and she suddenly didn't know what to do with her hands. Brushing past him, she headed to the counter to slice the cake.

"No," she replied as casually as she could. "The shop was exclusive and my allowance wasn't."

"Even with an employee discount?"

"Even so. I did buy a red slip, though. When I was a teenager, I saw *Gone With the Wind,* and Rhett Butler bought a red slip for Mammy. So I bought myself one and made believe Rhett Butler gave it to me."

He came up beside her to pour coffee into dark blue pedestal mugs. "While you were still a teenager?"

She sighed, remembering a time when she'd all but given up on Danny. "No," she said, carrying the plates to the table. "I'd been married five or six years, and Danny had spent the money I'd saved to put toward a house for a membership in a country club. He wanted to have better access to possible investors for his latest deal. In a fit of temper, I bought myself the slip."

He carried the cups to the table and said gently, "Kind of pathetic as paybacks go, considering what he'd done."

She nodded wryly. "I know. But I had to keep my head or we'd have been in the poorhouse by spring. So I allowed myself just a very small rebellion." She pulled out a chair and sat down. That was the point where Kara had begun to really give up on him. Before that, she'd been so sure she could save him, salvage the love they'd started out with and keep their little family together.

"Didn't work?" Cole asked, passing her the milk.

Kara shook her head. It had taken a year and a half—and an attempt at counseling—before she realized that Danny had no interest in looking out for his family. On his list, he was number one. After the real estate venture failed, Kara left the marriage and found a job teaching music in Courage Bay.

One day, if she got to know Cole better, she would tell him the sorry details of her marriage, but for now, she just said, "I stayed with Danny longer than I should have—for Taylor and me."

Cole picked up a slice of coffee cake that was redolent of orange and cinnamon and dotted with cranberries. Kara didn't have a lot of time to bake during the week, but she always kept a stash of her homemade treats in the freezer.

Cole sniffed the spicy aroma appreciatively, and she tried not to show her pride.

"Smells wonderful," he said, tactfully changing the subject. "How did you end up teaching hang gliding?"

"It was one of Danny's ventures," she told him, dismayed at how much of her life seemed to relate back to her ex. Taylor was the only wonderful thing to come out of that marriage. "I learned to 'fly' in order to help him out and keep costs down. I ended up running the place by myself for a few months when he lost interest and moved on to marketing video games. Or was it magnetic signs? Anyway, we finally sold the equipment to a local competitor." She gave a slightly embarrassed grin. "I just quit my job at Fly With Frank this morning. The thought that I might not have come home to Taylor last Saturday scared me."

Cole nodded. "Don't blame you. A single mother has to think about that." He took a bite of coffee cake. "Oh...Kara." His eyes closed, and when he opened them again, his expression was rapturous. "That's sinfully delicious. If anything could make me change my mind about getting married again, it would be food." He seemed to realize how that sounded and looked as if he wished he could take back the words.

"You don't cook at all?" she asked, deciding to rescue him.

"I can get by, but I never take the trouble. It's so much easier to get takeout or make a sandwich, or microwave something. And then my aunt has Brad's family and me over once a week." He pointed his fork at the cake on his plate. "It's this kind of thing that I miss—having something really special to eat. Especially when it's homemade."

"Thank you. Was your mother a good cook?"

"She was. Then, when she was no longer around to feed our stomachs and our souls, my aunt took over. Aunt Shirley's great with comfort foods. And she sprinkles her cooking liberally with advice on all sorts of things from my health to my love life—whether I'm hungry for it or not."

That sounded good to Kara. "It's nice to have someone who cares."

"Where's your family?" he asked. He took another bite of cake, rolling his eyes in pleasure.

She so enjoyed his reaction to her baking that it took her a moment to realize what he'd asked. "Uh…my parents are gone and I have no siblings, no cousins. I've made friends at school and they're wonderful, but not quite the same as family."

He nodded. "I know what you mean. I tease my aunt about butting into my life, but you're right. It reminds me that someone cares. And I have my brother, of course. Great guy. And my fellow officers are like a brotherhood for the most part."

"I imagine matters of life or death keep you pretty close. In my case, it's more sour notes and rambunctious behavior. We're allied for the kids, and we have a good principal."

"Loren Ford?" he asked, his expression skeptical.

She raised an eyebrow. "You know him?"

He nodded. "I went to high school with him. He was known for shooting down everyone else's ideas. We were on the student council together and it was hard to get anything accomplished when he was involved. He liked things done his way and only his way. And believe me, he wasn't always right."

She took offense to that assessment of Loren. "Maybe he was just a…a visionary. He's done very good things at the school…or so I hear."

"I didn't mean to disparage him," Cole said. "Maybe he's changed."

For some reason, his words didn't mollify her. "I don't know what he was like back in high school, but as far as I can tell, he's matured into a fine man and a good administrator."

"Ah," he said with a grin. "You have feelings for him."

She sat up a little straighter. "I do. Respect, admiration, and…and friendship."

"Hmm," he said, still watching her. He took another bite of her cake and swallowed. "And he wants more than that from you, doesn't he?"

That was true, and she wasn't sure why the fact that he'd guessed would annoy her, but it did. "Why would you think that?" she asked a little tightly.

He didn't seem to notice her pique. "Because it was typical behavior back then. He always hit on the pretty girls with the nurturing personalities, especially the ones taking home ec."

"You're afraid he's after me for my coffee cake?"

Kara had asked the question in jest, but Cole's only reaction was a tight smile.

"If he is," he finally replied, "would you give me an opportunity to better his offer?"

She was exhilarated and infuriated at the same time. "Like an auction?"

"No," he replied calmly. "But a vulnerable woman shouldn't be manipulated by a guy who's learned to deliver lines he thinks women want to hear. Or just…want."

She gasped indignantly. "Well, give me credit for some intelligence."

He nodded. "I do. But intelligence isn't what love is all about, is it."

"Who's talking about love?" she demanded. "He just asked me to the Christmas Ball. An invitation I refused, by the way. And how do you know how he treats women, anyway?"

"Word gets around. Let's just say Loren Ford looks out for number one."

Kara could not reconcile the school principal with the man Cole described. But guys probably had odd prejudices against each other that women didn't understand—power issues or old grudges.

On the one hand she was irritated by his remarks about Loren. And the fact she'd defended him probably affected Cole's opinion of *her.* On the other hand, she was surprised that he'd brought it up at all. Who she went out with didn't seem like something he should care about.

And whether he'd been teasing or not, he'd said he wanted a chance to "better Loren's offer." Hardly flattering stuff, but definitely an indication of interest.

She was considering how to respond when there was a large crash and the sound of shattering glass.

As she turned, wondering in alarm what on earth was happening, Cole leaned out of his chair and grabbed her arm, dragging her with him to the carpet. His hand cupped her head, pressing her face into his chest as the sound of glass tinkling seemed to go on and on.

When the noise finally stopped, she found that she

was lying on top of Cole. Fear, she noticed, was curiously absent in the sensory overload she was experiencing at such intimate contact with him. He, too, seemed unable to move for an instant. Then the cop in him must have taken over and, holding her head, he rolled them and got to his feet.

Kara turned her head toward the French doors and saw that the left one had a giant hole in it. Shards of jagged glass were everywhere.

"Taylor!" she cried suddenly, remembering that her son was out there somewhere.

"Stay down," Cole ordered, gesturing for her to remain on the carpet.

"But, Taylor—" she began, scrambling to her feet.

Suddenly Mel appeared at the jagged hole, looking longingly at the flat rock on the carpet, but smart enough not to venture over the broken glass.

Taylor appeared, his face framed by the hole, pale and horrified-looking.

Cole pushed himself to his feet and offered Kara a hand up. "Seems your son is the perp," he said dryly, "and not the victim. What happened, Taylor?"

Taylor looked at him, obviously frightened. "I...I lost the rubber bone somewhere in the bushes...." Taylor pointed behind him to a deep bank of rhododendron. "So...I found this flat rock, and Mel still had fun chasing it, only..." He turned his mortified expression on Kara. "I didn't mean to do it. I was aiming for the side of the house, but I...missed."

Kara was as horrified as her son. She couldn't imagine what replacing the glass would cost. She opened the intact door and pulled her son inside, putting a protective arm around him. "We'll pay to have it repaired, if you let us know who to call. And we'll clean up this—"

"I'll pay for it," Taylor said anxiously. "I've got that money you made me save from my birth—"

"Whoa." Cole stopped him with a hand on his shoulder.

Kara tightened her grip on her son, prepared to intercede if Cole was about to lecture Taylor on the wisdom of playing fetch with a rock. She would handle that part later.

"Don't tell me neither of you has ever broken a window before?" he said.

"Well...never someone else's," Taylor replied.

Kara was too surprised by Cole's smile, and the amiable tone of his voice to say anything.

"And that's a door," Taylor said. "A big one."

"Not a problem. I know someone who'll have it repaired by tonight."

"I'll pay—" Kara began.

"We'll talk about it when I get the bill." He pointed to a door in a small corridor off the kitchen. "Vacuum cleaner's in there. Want to get it? Don't touch the glass. I'll vacuum it up."

"Okay." Taylor hurried off, relieved to be able to do something about the mess he'd made.

Cole walked Mel inside, around the glass, then led him to the bedroom and closed the door.

Kara got down to pick up the bigger pieces of glass, but Cole caught her wrist to stop her.

"I'll do that," he said. "Come with me. You've got glass in your hair." He put a hand over her eyes and led her away. "Keep them closed."

"Where are we going?" she asked as she walked blindly beside him.

"To the bathroom," he replied. "Then I'm going to get the Dustbuster."

"Pardon me?"

"Sit down. I'll be right back." He pushed her down on what had to be the lid of the john, and Kara heard his retreating footsteps. Then he was back again.

"Did you say the Dustbuster?" she asked as she heard him move around her.

"Yes." He was standing behind her. He put a towel around her shoulders and removed the clip that held her hair up. She could feel his knee right beside her hip. "This is how the hospital gets glass out of the hair of victims of motor vehicle accidents."

Then the Dustbuster roared in her ears and she felt Cole's fingers comb carefully through her hair. She sat still under his ministrations, unable to believe this was happening to her. She barely knew Cole, but she'd started to fall in love with him on a perch in the Embrace. Now she was sitting in his bathroom while he worked her over with a Dustbuster!

He turned the machine off for a moment, running his fingers through her hair, and she took advantage of the silence.

"Thank you for not being angry," she said. "Taylor's never deliberately careless or destructive."

"I'm sure he isn't."

He lifted the hair up off her neck, apparently inspecting it. She could feel his breath against her skin.

"It was an accident," he said.

"You...probably...shouldn't eat the coffee cake on the table," she said, having a little difficulty focusing. "There could be glass in it."

"Okay—"

The roaring noise began again and she felt the little vacuum against her temples.

When he stopped again to move around her, she said quickly, "And you should empty the dog food bowl. There could be glass in it, too."

"Right." He vacuumed her hair a little longer, then handed Kara her purse, which he'd carried in with him. "Dig out your comb and I'll run it through your hair," he said. "Then we'll go over your sweater."

She did as he asked, and he combed gingerly through her now seriously disheveled hair. The proximity of his body to hers and the sensation created by his gentle ministrations were delightful. Pretending that she was unaffected was hard work.

The combing finished, he moved on to vacuum her shoulders and the back of her sweater. "You do the front," he said, handing her the machine, "while I check on Taylor and Mel."

Kara needed a moment to pull herself together. She stood alone in the now quiet bathroom, listening to the conversation taking place in the dining room. She drew a deep breath and expelled it raggedly. There was definitely something to be said for being the focal point of Cole Winslow's attention. This was the second time it had happened to her, and she was developing a real taste for it.

Taylor appeared in the doorway. "Mom? Are you okay?"

"I'm fine, Taylor," she assured him. "Did Cole clean up the glass?"

"Yeah. And guess what?" He was excited about something.

"What?"

"He says I can work off the cost of the door by exercising Mel! And I can come anytime."

"Really."

"Yeah. As long as he's home. Isn't that cool?"

It was. "Did you say thank you?"

Taylor rolled his eyes. He was doing that more and more lately.

"Yes, I said thank you." His expression brightened again. "I can't believe he wasn't *mad* about the door. Not even a little. I didn't do it on purpose, but it was really messy. And it's going to cost him *money*."

Money and the careful expenditure of it were well respected at their house.

"He understands you didn't mean to do it," she said. "Because he's a very nice man."

"Whew!" Taylor said expressively. "That's lucky for me."

And might not be bad for me, either, Kara thought. She carried the Dustbuster out into the living room, Taylor right behind her. Cole had finished with the standard vacuum. He'd let Mel out of the bedroom and was checking his paws. Judging by the way the dog wagged his tail and pretended to bite Cole's hand, Kara concluded his paws were glass-free.

Cole ruffled the dog's ears and let him go. "I'm happy to report that we have no casualties from the experience," he said, getting to his feet. "And the door will be replaced tonight."

"Is that going to cost you overtime?" Kara asked with a wince.

He shook his head. "I called a friend. I chose his security system and helped put it in, so all I have to do is pay for the glass. He'll provide the labor."

"Nice to have friends in the right places."

"Yes, it is."

"Again," she said with a sigh, "I'm so sorry, and I appreciate your being so nice about it. I'm accustomed to more dramatic types." Her husband had considered everything that went wrong a disaster.

Cole shrugged. "I see a lot of real tragedy. In the

scope of things, a little broken glass is of no real consequence."

His reaction was so wonderfully sane. The financially and emotionally treacherous world she'd occupied for so long seemed suddenly a bit brighter. She had to pay him back.

He put the vacuum cleaner back in its closet, and as he passed the stack of gifts, protected from the spray of glass by a little alcove, she had a sudden inspiration.

"What are you doing Saturday?" she blurted.

Cole glanced at Taylor, who was on the floor with Mel and completely occupied with a squeak toy. His eyebrow quirked up speculatively. "What did you have in mind?"

Ignoring the little riot his look caused inside her, she explained, "My choral group is wrapping gifts this weekend at the mall. I'm to be there all day Saturday and can have everything wrapped for you. My way of paying you back—at least, a little."

He smiled in appreciation. "Even the skis?"

"Even the skis. Though disguising them might be tricky."

"You're on," he said. "What time?"

"Anytime. I'll be there from ten to five."

"Wow. Long day."

She nodded. "The kids are great, but they need supervision, and it's a busy time of year to expect parents to help. We're trying to raise money to go to a choral competition in Seattle this spring."

"All right. I'll talk it up at the department."

"Cole..." Taylor sat back on his knees and scratched Mel's tummy, looked around in consternation. "Where's your Christmas tree?"

"A tree's a lot of trouble just for me," Cole replied. "I don't bother with one."

Taylor was aghast. "*No tree?* But it isn't Christmas without a tree. And where are you going to put the presents?"

"There's a tree at the station," Cole said reasonably, a little taken aback by Taylor's reaction. "It's all right. I mean, I don't really—"

"You *have* to have a tree!" Taylor insisted. "Where'll you put the stuff people bring you?"

"Well, I don't get that much—"

"'Cause you don't have a tree!"

Cole folded his arms, pretending to be serious when he was clearly amused. "So, that's what's doing it. I thought people just didn't like me." He turned to Kara. "What do you think?"

"Taylor's right," she said. "You should have a tree. The fragrance, the lights, the whole spirit of the thing is important to put you in the mood for the season."

He didn't want to rain on her parade, but in his experience, domestic violence and theft increased over the holidays, and observing the homeless was even more heartbreaking. It was sometimes hard for him to get in the Christmas spirit.

"There're trees at the mall," Taylor said helpfully. "Mom and I can help you find the perfect one."

"I don't have any ornaments."

"Mom's good at that. Aren't you, Mom."

Kara nodded. "And I owe you. I can share some ornaments, and my students are helping me make some for the music room. I might be able to sneak a few for you."

"OKAY, THEN." Cole didn't think much Christmas spirit could be sparked in him, but resisting Kara and Taylor's eagerness to help him would have been like kicking two of Santa's elves. "While you're wrapping, Taylor and I will find a tree," he told Kara. "And he can help me find a present for Blaine. Then, when you're finished for the day, you and Taylor can help me put up the tree."

"Good." Kara went to look over his pile of gifts.

She'd combed her hair into order, but Cole could still feel the silken threads of it in his fingers, smell the fresh fragrance of her shampoo. Being so close to her had reminded him of her rescue and made his heart race. It hadn't raced over a woman in years.

She turned to smile at him. "I might be able to get a tube for the skis from the furniture store in the mall. The rollers from carpets are sturdy and long enough, I think."

"Good idea."

"Well." She beckoned Taylor to her. "We'd better go. Thank you for the coffee. Don't forget to empty the dog dish."

"Right. You're welcome. Sure you don't want to take the rest of the cake home?"

"I'm sure. You enjoy it. And I'll see you Saturday."

"When can I start coming to exercise Mel?" Taylor asked.

"I've got swing shift the next few days, so I won't be home," Cole replied. "I'm off this weekend, then I'm on days all next week. How about Monday?"

Taylor looked disappointed. "That's four days away."

"But you'll see him Saturday," Kara reminded him.

The little boy's expression changed with flattering speed. "Oh, yeah. Okay." Taylor gave Mel a parting pat, then the dog followed Cole to the door.

"I'll come to the mall early Saturday," Cole said as he and Mel accompanied Kara and Taylor out to the sidewalk. "So you have plenty of time."

"I'll be ready." Kara put an arm around Taylor's shoulders and they headed to the corner, Taylor talking a mile a minute about Mel. They stopped to wave, and Cole waved back.

He waited on the sidewalk until they disappeared from sight. She'd be ready, Kara had said. Presumably she'd meant to wrap his gifts, but he'd detected an undercurrent in her words, and wondered if that was all she'd intended.

Because he wasn't sure *he* was ready, even though flirtatious remarks kept coming out of his mouth and he could scarcely look at her without remembering what it had felt like to have her pressed against him. Suddenly his imagination went to work on what it would be like to have her naked and in his arms.

He ran back into the house, Mel at his side as though they were on a job. He picked up the dog bowl and dumped the contents in the trash. After washing and drying it carefully, he ran his hand inside to make sure no tiny bits of glass had escaped him, then he refilled the bowl. Mel attacked the food as though he hadn't eaten in a week.

Cole felt like some sex-deprived adolescent who conjured up mental images of beautiful women. Except that wasn't the only way he thought about Kara. She was warm and maternal, but also brave and feisty…and fair. Most of all, she was fun to be with.

Suddenly warning bells seemed to go off in Cole's brain. What was happening here? A fantasy was fine. He just wasn't ready for anything else.

CHAPTER FIVE

"YOU'RE SURE BRAD wouldn't like a sweater-vest?" Shirley asked, as Cole filled her outstretched arms with all the light packages Brad had bought for Emily and was hiding at Cole's place. "A doctor should look distinguished even when he isn't on duty, then patients trust him. A sense of responsibility can be reflected in the clothes you wear."

"Really." Cole reached into the bed of his black Dodge Ram for a stack of heavier things. "I didn't know that. I didn't say he wouldn't like it. You should get him what you want to get him."

"But you gave me that look."

"What look?"

"The 'poor misguided fogy from another century' look. Are you telling me sweater-vests have gone out of fashion?"

"I haven't seen any recently."

She sighed as she marched beside him across the large parking lot and into the mall. Piped-in Christmas carols greeted them. At just after ten on a Saturday morning, the mall was already full of excited children and parents bracing for a marathon of shopping.

For the first time ever—including when he was married—Cole felt envious of these families who seemed so caught up in the holiday spirit. He stopped in his tracks, stunned by the realization.

Shirley halted beside him. "What is it, Cole?"

"Uh…just didn't want to run over that little girl." With one finger, he pointed at the toddler who'd just run across his path. "You keeping up?"

"Yes. Cute little thing, isn't she?" Shirley said, smiling in the direction of the child. "You could have a few of those if you got married again."

"Aunt Shirley…" he pleaded, falling into step beside her once more.

"The fact that you don't want to talk about it doesn't make it a taboo subject, you know." She grinned affectionately at him.

"Do you want to walk home?" he threatened.

"The girls are taking me home after we have lunch. I'd intended to buy your present today, but that's questionable now."

"The girls" were three women around Shirley's age. They called themselves the Courage Bay Grannies and were very involved in fund-raising and community action.

Cole spotted Kara at a long table set up against one wall. She was laboring over a package while Taylor spun a spool of ribbon on one finger. A stack of boxes was piled at one end of the table, along with a two-roll paper cutter.

Taylor spotted Cole and raced toward him, taking the plastic bag dangling from his fingers. "Hi, Cole!" he said, sounding glad to see him. He was probably already bored and looking forward to a little action—even if it involved shopping.

"Hi, Taylor." Cole introduced his aunt. "Shirley lives just about a block from you."

Taylor politely shook her hand. "Mom's already made twelve dollars!" He seemed to consider that a small fortune. "And she got a carpet roller to wrap your brother's skis in."

"That's great."

"Hi!" Kara walked over and greeted them warmly, then helped Cole place his packages behind the table.

Cole introduced his aunt to Kara, and mentioned that Shirley was a good friend of Candy Lester, Gehlen's mother, who volunteered in the principal's office.

"Candy's one of my favorite people," Kara enthused. "I had no idea she was Gehlen's mother."

It had always been Cole's theory that Gehlen hiked and climbed in an effort to escape his mother. Candy's hair was dyed blond, she wore false eyelashes at seventy-something, and her favorite item of clothing was a fuchsia baseball cap covered in rhinestones.

Moments later Shirley excused herself to meet her friends. As she bustled away into the crowd, Kara said, "What a lovely lady."

"That she is," Cole agreed.

"Where's Mel?" Taylor asked.

"I left him home," Cole replied. "He doesn't like crowds." He turned to Kara. "Can I do anything to help? I hate to leave you with all this."

She handed him a pad of sticky notes. "Yes, you can put a note on each package with the name of the recipient, so that once it's wrapped, I can put the note back on and you'll know who it's for."

"Right." He took the pen she offered. "I forgot all about that."

"It's okay. I have to remind everyone."

She looked like a carefree teenager this morning. She was wearing a festive snowman vest, and her hair was caught up in a high ponytail tied with a red-and-green plaid bow. She pushed her chair out for him to sit on.

While Cole was writing names on notes, two students arrived to help with the wrapping. The boy, Jared, was tall and had a lot to say. He seemed a little smooth for his age, though he did jump right in and help without being asked. Amy, on the other hand, was shy-looking. She was carrying a can of pop and a bag from the bakery.

"I brought old-fashioned glazed donuts for everyone," she said, holding up the bag. "But I didn't know what you'd want to drink."

"Taylor and I'll get drinks for you before we go shopping," Cole volunteered, the notes finally finished. "What do you want, Kara?"

"A caramel mocha," she replied, rubbing her hands together in anticipation. "With whipped cream, please. Jared?"

"A double cap, skinny, dash of cinnamon," Jared ordered without looking up from the package he wrapped. "And thank you."

"You're welcome." Cole took off with Taylor, thinking that when an eighth grade boy knew his way around a coffee bar, the world was growing too sophisticated for a simple cop with lowbrow tastes.

Cole put a hand on Taylor's shoulder as they made their way through the crowd.

"Can we go see the train?" Taylor asked, pointing to a small locomotive making its way around an animated display of Santa's workshop.

"Let's get the coffee like I promised, then we'll go check that out."

At the coffee bar, Cole placed the order, then headed to the far end of the counter to pick it up. When he turned to say something to Taylor, the boy was gone.

Cole refused to be alarmed. Kids took off exploring all the time.

He turned in the direction of the locomotive, sure he'd spot Taylor right away. But he wasn't there.

Cole scanned the long corridor of the mall. The shopping center now teemed with people, men, women and children rushing from store to store, up and down escalators. A child could become lost—or worse—so quickly.

Fear, swift and powerful, surged through Cole. This was different from facing down a gun. That kind of situation kick-started your adrenaline and brought your training to the fore.

This just brought cold, heavy dread.

He did the only thing he could think of. He shouted "Taylor!" in a loud, authoritative voice.

"Yeah?" Taylor asked.

Cole looked down to see Taylor at his side. "Where did you come from?" Cole demanded, his voice a little raspy.

"San Francisco," Taylor replied seriously.

All Cole's internal alert systems settled down to normal. "I mean," he corrected patiently, "where did you come from just now?"

"I was right here," Taylor replied a little anxiously, as though afraid he was in trouble. He pointed to a rack of pastries. "I was standing over there, looking at the brownies."

Enormously relieved, Cole realized he hadn't asked Taylor if he wanted anything to eat. "Do you want one?"

Taylor brightened. "Yeah, please."

"And a milk?"

"Can I have cocoa?"

"Sure." He bought the brownie and cocoa and handed them to Taylor. "Stay with me, okay? Your mom wouldn't like it if I lost you."

Taylor laughed as he took a giant bite of brownie.

"She'd get in a blue snit," he said, as soon as he could speak.

Cole slowed his pace so that Taylor could keep up. "What's a blue snit?"

"It's when she loses her temper and has to lock herself in her room so she won't give me back to the junk man."

Cole laughed. "That doesn't sound like a good thing."

They delivered the coffee, and Kara noticed the half-eaten brownie in Taylor's hand.

"Did you say thank you?" she asked her son.

Taylor looked momentarily worried. "I think I did."

"You did," Cole assured him. "Anything we can pick up for you while we're shopping?" he asked Kara.

She shook her head. "Thanks, but I'm going to do my shopping next weekend when Jared's mother can cover the wrapping for me."

"Okay, then." He turned to Taylor, who had finished the brownie. "You ready?"

"Yeah." Taylor hurried to keep up with him as he started out for the Santa display.

"You want to stand in line and tell Santa what you want?" Cole asked.

Taylor looked up at him in surprise as he dodged a stroller. "No. I just want to see the train. It's got this cool flatcar with all kinds of trucks on it."

"You sure you don't want to see Santa?" Cole asked. "I don't mind waiting."

Taylor stopped walking and stared up at Cole under

the vaulted glass dome in the middle of the mall. His expression was very serious. "You know he isn't real, right?"

Cole struggled to remain just as serious. "Who? Santa?"

"Yeah. All the Santas you see in stores aren't really his helpers. They're just people who act like Santa so little kids will believe."

Cole was surprised and a little disappointed in the boy's conviction. "I thought he was real," he argued.

Taylor studied him uncertainly, then punched him in the arm. "No, you didn't!"

"Yes, I did," Cole insisted. "Every Christmas I've gotten presents I wanted but didn't ask for."

"That's your mom," Taylor confided.

"I don't have a mom."

"Then it's your dad."

"He's been gone since I was ten."

Taylor drew a breath. "There's no Santa, Cole. Somebody who loves you is doing it. I bet it's your aunt."

"Then...she's acting like Santa, even though it isn't her job. That's all the real Santa does—gives you stuff to make you happy."

"But only if you've been good," Taylor added, then apparently realizing he was being drawn into the myth, he sighed again. "At least, that's how the story goes. Adults just use Santa to make you be good."

Cole wasn't sure why it was important to him that this eight-year-old believe in Santa. Somehow it just seemed criminal that Taylor had a father who thought more of his scams than his son, and a mother who felt it necessary to lie about his father rather than say he was in jail. Taylor had been uprooted from his home and was having trouble making new friends. He should have something to believe in that would make this Christmas special.

Cole put a hand on his shoulder and drew the boy closer. "Well, fortunately, I've been excellent this year. What about you?"

Taylor nodded enthusiastically. "You have been excellent. You saved my mom's life." His expression grew troubled as they set off toward the train. "I haven't been so good. Sometimes...sometimes I'm not very nice to Mom."

Should he be venturing into this territory? Cole wondered. But the child was confiding in him. It was hard to back away. "Why not?"

"'Cause she made my dad go away."

Oh-oh. The unwritten rules were clear. He could listen, but he couldn't offer an opinion. "Why do you think that?"

"Because he'd come back if Mom let him. She used to yell at him a lot."

"Why do you suppose that was?"

"I don't know. Money, I think. Anyway, he joined the army. He's somewhere safe. I think Germany. But he's not coming back because Mom divorced him."

"Oh."

"Yeah. Some soldiers get to come home, but he doesn't. That's 'cause he's doing something special. The army needs him all the time."

"I see."

They had reached the Santa display, and Taylor was instantly distracted by the action as the train clacked by, whistle blowing, glittery smoke billowing out, animated elves and reindeer waving from the passenger car windows. In one car, gifts were piled high; another was filled with candy canes and ribbon candy, and as Taylor had said, the flatcar carried a flamboyant collection of service trucks and a snowplow.

Cole was grateful for the distraction. He didn't have a clue how to advise Taylor. Then he remembered he didn't have the right to try.

They watched the train make several circuits, then Taylor turned to Cole, the grim expression gone from his face. "That was cool. You want to go to the toy store to find something for your neighbor?"

"Yes. You seen enough of the train?"

"Can we come back again? Before I have to help Mom?"

"Sure."

They checked out the toy section of a department store, then two other toy stores before finding the Air Athletes that Blaine's parents had said were on Blaine's list. The toys were a type of transformer that could be turned from aircraft into sports heroes with the manipulation and addition of parts.

Cole picked one up to examine it.

"Not that one," Taylor said, choosing another and handing it to him. "*This* one."

"What's the difference?"

"The one you picked is a galaxy freighter that turns into a baseball player."

"Sounds cool."

Taylor looked at him as though he were to be pitied. He placed his hand on the box he'd given Cole. "This one's a Gamma Quadrant patrol ship and turns into a quarterback!" That information imparted, he waited anxiously for Cole's reaction.

Cole wasn't getting it. "And that's better?"

"Well, yeah. It patrols—it doesn't just haul freight. And quarterbacks get more babes than baseball players."

Cole was momentarily stunned. That was a standard of choice for eight-year-olds?

"How do you know that, if you don't like sports?" he asked.

"That's what the kids at school say."

"Well, maybe guys believe that in school," Cole disputed, tucking the box under his arm, "but in *real* life, I think Sammy Sosa does okay with women."

"Well, I like that one, and you said Blaine's like me."

What better endorsement could he ask for? Cole thought.

"Can you help me buy something for my mom?" Taylor asked as they left the shop after making the purchase.

"Uh...sure. But I'm not much of an expert on what women like."

"Don't you have a girlfriend?"

"Not at the moment, no."

"Did you ever have any?"

"Yeah, I've had girlfriends," Cole told him. "But no one special."

Taylor seemed pleased at the state of Cole's love life, but his next words made Cole uneasy.

"I'm glad my mom doesn't have a boyfriend, 'cause I know my dad's coming back someday." Before Cole could say anything, Taylor pointed to a jewelry store. "Can we look in there?"

"We can look," Cole said, starting off in that direction, "but there might not be anything you can afford. There's nothing in there *I* can afford, and I've got a job."

Taylor laughed and peered in the window at the sparkling gold and diamonds with large price tags.

"Whoa!" Taylor exclaimed in mingled horror and amazement. "They're sure pretty, though."

"I agree." Cole spotted a kitchen shop farther down. "Since your mom likes to bake, what about something for the kitchen?"

"Like what?"

"I'm not sure. But you'll probably know when you see it."

The Kitchen Cabinet was small but stuffed with everything imaginable for people who liked to cook.

"Roosters!" Taylor exclaimed, heading toward a little nook where everything displayed had a rooster theme. "Mom loves roosters. She has them all over the kitchen."

His hands reached up to a pair of rooster candleholders. A tall green candle stood in each one. "She loves candles, too!" Taylor said, his eyes gleaming. He lifted one of the roosters to check under it for the price.

Cole caught the candle before it fell to the floor.

"Thanks," Taylor said with a big grin. "And I have enough money! They're seven ninety-five each and I have seventeen dollars!"

"Perfect." Taylor was pushing it with the tax, but Cole didn't say anything. This was probably a good lesson in shopping. Cole checked the price on a teapot decorated with a hand-painted rooster, while Taylor went to the counter.

"That'll be twenty-two dollars and forty-two cents," the sales clerk said pleasantly. "Would you like me to wrap it for you?"

Taylor was silent for a moment. "But the price tag says seven ninety-five each. That's only...fifteen-ninety."

The clerk sounded apologetic. "The candles are extra, sweetie. They're two-fifty a piece. Then there's seven-and-a-quarter percent sales tax."

Taylor's shoulders fell. "I always forget about the tax."

Cole walked to the counter.

"How about if I lend you the extra?" he said to Taylor, offering him a ten-dollar bill.

"But I already owe you...." Taylor looked at the bill but didn't take it.

"We'll just tack it on to the price of the door."

"Mom'll get mad at me for letting you give me stuff."

"If she does, I'll explain." He handed the bill to the clerk. "Can you wrap it for him?"

"I can," she said, clearly pleased at the outcome. She headed for a table at the back of the store, then returned in a few minutes with the finished product in a craft-paper gift bag with handles, the front emblazoned with the shop's name in pink and purple.

While they'd been waiting for her, Taylor had found a spinning rack of small specialty ornaments. "Here's Mel," he said, removing a dog-shaped ornament with Mel's markings and handing it to Cole. "You should get that if you're going to buy a tree today."

Cole looked through the rack and found an angel with a harp, perfect for Kara, and Santa on a train for Taylor. He paid for all three, then kept the dog and gave the other two to Taylor.

"Thanks!" Taylor said. "The angel is for Mom, right?"

"Right."

"You're trying to be a Santa, aren'tcha?" Taylor asked as they left the store. "Giving people stuff to make them happy."

"Well, your mom's doing a nice thing for me. She's wrapping all my presents. And you're okay to hang out with."

Taylor looked heartbreakingly pleased. "Thanks," he said.

"You're welcome. Let's check in with your mom and then we'll get some lunch."

"Can we go to Tully's Restaurant? They have chili fries and chocolate monster sundaes."

"You're not going to get sick all over me, are you?"

"No. Mom says I have an iron constitution."

That proved to be true. After a mild protest that Taylor was taking too much of Cole's time, Kara gave Taylor money for lunch. The gift-wrap table was swamped with customers, so she waved the two of them off before disappearing into a sea of paper and ribbon.

Taylor had two orders of chili fries, two large pops and the monster sundae. "No, I have to pay for it," he said when Cole took care of the bill and pushed his money back toward him. "Mom'll be mad. She'll think I wanted to keep the money for myself."

"Then buy her something extra for Christmas," Cole suggested. "And just don't tell her I bought your lunch." Then, realizing he was encouraging the boy to lie to his mother, he corrected quickly, "I mean, don't volunteer anything. If she asks about lunch, let me do the talking."

Taylor took a sip of pop and shook his head. "Mom finds out everything," he said finally. "I don't know how she does it, but she does."

Cole could believe that. He imagined Kara's life

was difficult, having to support a child on her own and manage other people's children all day. But she seemed to be doing a very good job at both.

Except for telling Taylor his father was in the military. That seemed wrong to Cole, but then, he wasn't the person responsible for Taylor's emotional welfare.

And why was he worrying about it, anyway? he asked himself impatiently. He was just keeping the boy entertained while his mother was doing a favor for Cole. He had no personal stake in this, much as he liked both Kara and her son.

Well, *like* was an insipid word for the way he felt about her, but his need to keep his life emotionally uncomplicated was proportionately strong. He'd just go with that.

Taylor spotted a pet shop with tabby kittens in the window, all sporting big red bows. Catching Cole's hand, he dragged him over to have a look, then pleaded to go inside and see the puppies.

Unable to refuse, aware of the need in the boy's eyes and in the hand that held his, Cole allowed himself to be hauled inside.

So much for keeping his life uncomplicated.

CHAPTER SIX

"MOM, WE HAVE TO HELP Cole buy his tree! He's never bought one before, and he won't know what to get. He might buy a dinky little one and ruin the whole thing!" Taylor was adamant that the moment Kara closed up the wrapping table, they had to accompany Cole to the front of the mall where the Boy Scouts were selling Christmas trees.

"Honey," she said patiently, "Cole's had you with him most of the day. I'm sure he needs some quiet time."

"But he *asked* us to help him," Taylor explained. "He's never bought a tree by himself since he lived at home."

She should tell a white lie and say they had too much to do at home, but she didn't. Straightforward by nature, Kara dealt with young teens all day; nothing but honesty worked with them.

"We'll be happy to help you if you want help," she offered.

"I do," Cole said. "But I was just going to get a small tree for the top of the table." He winked at Kara, apparently aware that the notion of a small tree would drive Taylor wild. "One of those two-foot artificial—"

Taylor rose to the bait. "No! See, Mom! We have to help him." To Cole, he said patiently, "Nothing fake, and it has to be tall enough so you can smell it upstairs."

"I don't have an upstairs."

"Well, everywhere in your house, then. And it has to hold lots of lights and ornaments. That makes you feel good when you look at it."

That one surprised Kara. She'd despaired of Taylor ever feeling good again. His whole demeanor seemed different since he'd gone shopping with Cole. She was afraid to hope that life was returning to normal—that Taylor would be happy and trust her again, the way he used to.

Cole nodded gravely at Kara. "I guess it's clear you have to help with this. When are you going to be finished here?"

"Another hour, at least," Kara replied. "We can meet you out front then."

He gathered up the packages she'd finished for him. There were still several more to go. "I'll put these in the truck," Cole told her, "then I've got a little more shopping to do and I'll be back in time to help you pack up."

"If you're sure…"

"I'm sure. Taylor, see you later."

"Can I come?" Taylor asked hopefully.

"You promised to help *me*," Kara said, certain Cole

needed a break from her suddenly gregarious son. She squeezed his shoulder to soften the disappointment.

"But this is so *boring*," he whined dramatically.

"If you'd help out, it wouldn't be. Here, put bows on all those boxes. And make sure the sticky notes stay with them, so we know who they belong to." She waved Cole off. "We'll see you in an hour or so."

He hesitated. "You need another coffee before I go?"

"No, I'm good. Thank you."

As she watched him walk away, Kara told herself that Christmas tree shopping could hardly be considered a date. But she felt inside as though she'd been invited to dinner and dancing.

Taylor gave her a minute-by-minute account of his day with Cole as he placed bows on packages with careful precision. "We saw the train at the place where Santa talks to the little kids. Cole told me he believes in Santa Claus. Do you think he does?"

When Kara looked up at him, not quite sure how to answer, Taylor did it for her. "I think he was just kidding. He wants me to believe. Cole helped me buy your present, Mom." He glanced at her tauntingly. "Want me to tell you what it is?"

Kara had a terrible need-to-know where Christmas gifts were concerned. Gifts that came early were opened on the spot. She couldn't stand to see an unopened present. And she was never disappointed Christmas morning when there was nothing to open, because she'd had such fun before.

But now that Taylor was growing up, she tried hard not to pass that habit on to him.

"I'd rather be surprised," she lied, running the edge of her scissors along a length of red ribbon.

"Good," he said, "'cause I wasn't gonna tell you. Cole says nobody should open presents until Christmas Eve."

"Really." Kara was happy that Taylor seemed to like Cole, but no way would she let either of them influence this particular tradition.

"We bought a new chew toy for Mel at the pet store," he went on, relentlessly applying bows. "We had *lots* of stuff for lunch, and he didn't make me get anything healthy or tell me to have an apple instead of a sundae. I like that. And he let me do my own shopping. He just came to help when I didn't have enough…money." Taylor had been chattering on, but that last word was added lamely as he glanced guiltily at her.

"For what?" she asked, afraid she knew the answer. "For my present? Oh, Taylor, I told you I didn't want—"

"I didn't get anything big!" He raised both hands and took a step back, as though arguing with her required a little distance. "I found something *perfect,* but I forgot…well, I needed a little more money, so Cole lent me some. I'm gonna work hard, Mom, don't worry."

"Honey, I know you intend to, but when you borrow from me, you forget—"

"This is between him and me," Taylor interrupted. "I'll pay him back. I promised." He picked up a soccer ball that had been left to wrap. "I think Dad's going to like him."

So, Kara thought. Cole was Taylor's friend and therefore not a threat to his dream of a reunion between her and Danny.

"Taylor, your father and I are divorced," she said quietly but with firmness. "He's not coming back."

"He might come back to see me," he insisted. "And when he does, I think he'd like Cole."

"Everybody probably likes Cole," she conceded. She handed him a box for the ball. "Put that in here and stuff some tissue around it so..."

Of course, he had to toss it as she spoke. Jared, who was coming back from a brief break, reached to catch it in midair, but he lost control of it and it went sailing into the crowd of shoppers.

Jared and Taylor took off in laughing pursuit, and the next thing she knew, the runaway ball—and the kids—were on the down escalator. She wanted desperately to follow, but couldn't leave the gifts unattended. She prayed fervently that the ball wouldn't trip anyone.

A few minutes later, Jared and Taylor reappeared on the up escalator, looking grim. Kara felt a moment's panic, afraid to think what might have happened, then she spotted Loren Ford behind them, the ball tucked under his arm. They marched in a column to her table.

"Tell me that you were wrapping this for someone," Loren said as he approached her, "and that our students were *not* playing soccer with it in the middle of the mall."

"Did it hit anyone?" she asked anxiously, taking the ball and checking for smudges.

"No," Jared said quickly. "We caught it right at the bottom of the escalator."

Kara felt great relief. "It escaped," she explained to Loren with a reasonable smile. "We were putting it into a box and it…got away from us. I sent the kids after it."

Loren handed the ball to Kara. "Well, that's comforting. I wouldn't want to read in the paper that we'd knocked a shopper unconscious."

"No, sir." Jared took the ball from her, and he and Taylor went to wrap it. Then, with skills a diplomat might envy, he encouraged Kara, "Tell him how well we're doing, Mrs. Abbott."

A perfect diversion, Kara thought. "We've made a little over two hundred dollars," she said, pointing to the cash box stashed under the table. "Next weekend should be even better."

He nodded his approval. "Good work," he said. "I guess you'll be taking it easy once you get home tonight."

Taylor looked up, his expression eager. "We've got a date," he piped up.

Loren put his hands in the pockets of his tailored

leather jacket, his forehead furrowed. "A date? I thought you weren't interested in dating."

"It's not really a—" Kara began, but Taylor interrupted.

"We're going to help Cole buy a Christmas tree. Cole likes Mom and me."

Loren looked a bit confused and none too pleased. "Who is Cole? Not...?"

"I'm right here," Cole said suddenly, joining them with an armload of packages that he placed on the table. He offered his hand to Loren. "And yeah, it's me. Small world, huh?"

Loren stiffened slightly but he shook Cole's hand. "Well," he said. "It's been a long time, Winslow."

"Cole saved Mom's life when she was stuck in the tree." Taylor was beaming up at Cole. "She would've died if Cole and Mel hadn't saved her. Mel's a German shepherd and he's really great."

Loren nodded. "Yes. Your mom told me and I also read about it in the paper." He turned to Cole. "You're quite the hero."

Cole shrugged. "All in a day's work. If you ask me, keeping all those kids in order at school is pretty heroic."

Kara thought that was a considerate thing to say, but Loren only seemed annoyed.

"Hardly the same, though, is it?" he asked grimly. "Gives you the edge when it comes to women."

Kara saw something subtle change in Cole's eyes. "I've never really noticed."

The atmosphere became charged.

"Come on, Loren," Kara teased. "A man who can deal with kids has a major appeal for women. Taylor, let Jared finish wrapping that and you help me pack up." She pulled out the cash box and handed it to Loren. "You want to take care of this?"

"I guess I'd better," he said, "since you're not going right home. See you Monday." He walked away.

She wasn't sure why Loren's behavior made her annoyed with him, Taylor and Cole, but it did. "He is very good with the kids, you know."

Cole picked up the heavy roll of wrap. "Why did you turn down his invitation to the Christmas Ball?"

"Because I didn't want to go with him," she replied, dropping odds and ends in a box and handing the box to Taylor.

"Why not? You said women find his type appealing."

"I can appreciate his work without being attracted to him." She handed him her car keys. "Thanks," she said a little stiffly. "As soon as Jared's finished, I'll fold up the table."

Kara hadn't exactly been honest with Cole, but she knew he wasn't ready to hear the truth yet. I've known you just a week, Cole Winslow, but you're the answer to my prayers. Why would I be interested in anyone else?

CHAPTER SEVEN

COLE BOUGHT an eight-foot grand fir. It was long-needled, beautifully shaped and very fragrant. Kara and Taylor had dragged him through the entire lot, skipping the rows with trees under five feet, and pointing out the advantages of the different types. Kara showed Cole how to bend the needle to determine how fresh the tree was. Then she made sure he took each tree he was interested in and stood it up, turning it to check for bald spots or short branches. The lot smelled like heaven.

"A lot of people like blue spruce," she said, "because of the space between the branches, but I prefer Scotch pine. They're so bushy you don't see the wires from the lights. And by the time Christmas comes, you get some natural spacing anyway, since the tree opens up as it dries."

"You ever think about becoming a Christmas tree farmer?" he asked her as they hauled the grand fir to the trailer to pay.

She shook her head. "I don't know a thing about growing them—just decorating them. Christmas was so special for my friends and their families when I was a child, and my grandmother always made me something special. But my parents never fussed over the holidays. I want Taylor to have the kind of Christmas I always wanted."

"He's definitely hot on getting just the right tree," Cole told her.

Taylor was intently studying a twelve-footer that was probably headed for the lobby of an office building.

"I don't know what the two of you did today," Kara said, "but he's so enthused. Thank you for spending so much time with him."

"I had a good time, too," he said, rapping on the door of the trailer. "He's a great kid. Your husband's a jerk for hurting him like that."

She nodded. "That's what finally made me leave. I could have tried to save our marriage until our fiftieth anniversary, but that wouldn't have done Taylor any good."

"I don't think he's mad at you anymore. He took great pains finding you just the right Christmas gift."

Her expression became playfully threatening. "Incidentally, don't fill his head with that 'nothing should be opened before Christmas' nonsense. I mean, it's okay for him, but I want to be free to peek whenever I feel like it."

"You're welcome to," he said, "but that puts you on the naughty list—doesn't bode well for Santa's visit."

After Cole paid for the tree, the lot attendant tied it

up and helped Cole put it in the back of his truck. "Thanks," he said as he headed off toward another customer. "Hope your family has a great holiday."

Your family. The words did have a certain appeal.

"What are your thoughts on broccoli beef?" Cole asked Kara, not wanting to examine the thought more closely.

She studied him a moment, then smiled. "Well, it's a complicated issue," she said.

"No, it's not," Taylor announced. "Broccoli is definitely yucky."

"I like it—" she said, anticipation lighting her eyes.

It was obvious to him that she was pleased with the invitation. He liked her lack of artifice.

"—with a side order of pan-fried noodles instead of rice, and a spring roll."

When she smiled at him like that, he'd get her anything she wanted.

"Oh, no," Taylor complained. "Let's get burgers, barbecue, fried chicken—*anything* else but broccoli!"

Cole looked to Kara for a decision.

"I love Chinese food," she replied. "Shall we meet you there?"

"No, pile in with me," he said, opening the passenger door. "I'll bring you back to your car. We put all your wrap and stuff in the trunk and locked it up, so it should be safe."

She urged Taylor in ahead of her. "Then let's go."

Cole drove to an industrial area on the outskirts of

Courage Bay. A few lights were strung around the Esmee Engines plant as a concession to Christmas, and a fleet of trucks lined the asphalt outside the warehouse.

Taylor pointed to the semitrailers. "That's what I'm going to do when I grow up!" he said. "Drive a big rig all the way across the country."

"That's a good job," Cole agreed. "You get to be your own boss on the road."

"I'd drive *that* one!" Taylor pointed to a red truck with a big dog painted on the driver's door. "Only, I'd put Mel's picture on the door."

Taylor continued to make plans about his future in long-haul trucking until Cole pulled into the parking lot of the Chinese restaurant. Once inside, the boy's high spirits slipped at the prospect of unpalatable food.

Taylor sat on Cole's side of the booth while Kara and Cole ordered. The little boy refused a menu, insisting there was nothing on it he'd like. But he placated his mother by telling her he'd microwave her leftover chicken when he got home.

Cole ordered a selection of appetizers, certain something would tickle Taylor's appetite.

When the platter arrived, Taylor sat up, mildly interested. Cole put a spring roll on his plate and pushed the sweet sauce toward him. "Try that," he encouraged. "Dip it in the red stuff, but be careful of the yellow—it's hot." What kid wouldn't respond to the challenge that he couldn't handle hot mustard?

Cole and Kara were talking about her choral group when Taylor began to choke. A large dollop of hot mustard on his plate told the tale. Cole handed him a glass of water, then a fried shrimp to help kill the taste.

"I don't think I like seafood," Taylor said in a raspy voice.

"Everybody likes this. Try it. Dip it in the red stuff."

When he'd eaten the shrimp along with several more spring rolls, Taylor leaned toward the crab puffs. "What are those?"

"Crab puffs."

"More seafood?"

"Yeah. But you liked the shrimp, right? Would I steer you wrong?"

Picking one up, Taylor examined it. "I'm supposed to dip it in the red stuff?"

"Right."

He did that and popped it into his mouth, grinned, then reached for another one.

Rats, Cole thought. The kid liked everything he liked. He'd have to buy another round.

AS SHE WATCHED HER SON demolish the appetizer plate, Kara made a decision. It didn't matter what reservations Cole had about getting married again; she was going to help him get over them. Taylor needed Cole as much as she did.

"I have an extra Christmas tree stand," she said conversationally, keeping her newfound resolve to herself. "I thought I'd lost mine when we moved here, so I bought another one, then the old one turned up in a box in the basement. I also have a Christmas tree skirt if you need one."

"A what?" he asked, puzzled.

"A tree skirt." She made a circle in the air with her fork. "You know, it goes under the tree and you put the presents on it."

"Ah. That. I thought you just used an old bedsheet."

"Well, that'd work, too, but if you want to get serious about decorating, a tree skirt is a must. I have my mother's, and the one I made for my hope chest. I'll lend you one. Just wait—we'll have your house so filled with Christmas cheer you'll feel like Santa himself."

"He is like Santa!" Taylor said, reaching into the pocket of his jacket. He removed a small brown bag, dug into it and handed her a glittery little angel on a gold string. "He bought this for you, 'cause you wrapped all his presents."

It was a pretty little angel with a shiny white dress, frothy dark hair and a thin wire halo. A tiny harp was in her hands. "She's beautiful," Kara said, frowning at Cole, "but I wrapped your presents because you were so kind about Taylor breaking the door. I was trying to pay *you* back."

"That's not exactly a payback," he said, pointing to the angel in her hand. "I just saw it and thought you should have it."

"He bought me one, too." Taylor pulled another ornament out of the sack, this one of Santa waving from the engine of a train.

Kara took the decoration from him to admire, then handed it back. "Thank you," she said to Cole. "That was very thoughtful, though not surprising in someone who believes in Santa."

Cole turned to Taylor. "You ratted me out."

"It's okay." Kara attached her angel to the strap of her purse. "I'm a believer, too. Taylor is skeptical, but he'll come around."

Taylor looked from one to the other in confusion. "Mom," he said, finally focusing on her. "There's no Santa. It's just the spirit of…of…"

Kara helped him out. "Love and generosity. The spirit of Santa. That makes everyone who believes in those things a sort of Santa."

He nodded his head in amazement. "That's what Cole said." He leaned companionably toward Cole. "Do you have garland and lights? You gotta have those, too."

"No," Cole replied. "But I can pick some up tomorrow. You want to come help me put all this together?"

"Yeah!" Taylor answered for them, allowing Kara to pretend to have to think about it. "Mom's the best at it! Huh, Mom?"

Kara couldn't remember the last time her son had called her "the best"—even if it was only at decorating a Christmas tree.

"I am pretty good." She feigned nonchalance. "We'd love to help if you can take our company two days in a row."

The look he sent her was decidedly sexual, yet filled with something else as well. It told her he appreciated her…wanted more of her. Her heartbeat accelerated.

"Well, today was pretty tough," Cole joked, passing her the small plate of fortune cookies. "Someone wrapped all my gifts, I had a personal shopper at the toy store, and that same person kept me company over lunch, and tonight he helped me keep my weight down by eating half my dinner." He laughed as Taylor elbowed him. "I think I could handle another day of the Abbotts."

"Then we're yours," Kara said. Realizing how wistful she sounded, she added quickly, "For tomorrow, at least."

She snapped open her fortune cookie and read aloud. "All good things come to those who are patient." Dropping the little ribbon of paper into her purse, she prayed that was true.

Cole drove them back to the mall parking lot, which was almost empty now. He pulled his truck up beside her little silver compact and got out.

"Don't worry, we'll be fine," she insisted, but he didn't seem to be listening. She unlocked the car doors and Taylor climbed into the back seat, then Cole pulled her door open. She turned to him to say good-night, and without warning he put a hand to the back of her head, the other around her waist, and drew her to him.

He seemed about to say something. Then, with an abbreviated shake of his head, he changed his mind and kissed her.

Taken by surprise, she opened her mouth and her arms. He pulled her against him, and she realized how powerful and strong he was. The same thrill of recognition and sensual awareness that she'd felt as he'd held her on the edge of the Embrace washed through her. The promise of both physical and emotional safety.

His mouth on hers was tender, yet bold—just like the man himself, she thought, before giving herself over to the experience.

Cole's a happy bachelor, an annoying little voice prodded her. He was just giving a good-night kiss to a woman he'd enjoyed spending time with.

But the way his body bent protectively over hers didn't feel at all casual. And the kiss was impassioned and purposeful.

When he raised his head, she saw affection in his eyes.

"What time tomorrow?" he asked.

"Time," she repeated, forcing herself down to earth. "How about eleven? I can bring lunch."

"I'll take you and Taylor out somewhere."

"No, once we start decorating we won't want to lose our momentum. Okay?"

"Okay."

Forcing herself to leave his arms, she climbed in behind the wheel of her car. She felt as though she could make it fly.

Cole leaned in, said good-night to Taylor, then whispered, "Good night, Kara," in a way that suggested he didn't want to leave. "I'll follow you home."

"That's not..." she began, but again, he wasn't listening. He'd climbed into the truck and was waiting for her to pull out.

Thrilled over that kiss and his gentle attentions, she turned the key in the ignition, laughing lightly to herself. She directed a smile at Taylor—who looked back at her as though she'd just slapped him.

"Why did you *do* that?" he demanded, his eyes brimming with tears.

How on earth did a mother explain sexual attraction to an eight-year-old?

She stepped lightly on the accelerator and drove to the exit. "Because our friendship is special," she said carefully, trying to sound as though she knew what she was talking about. "And when adults feel that special friendship, they sometimes kiss as a way to...to communicate it."

"But you're married to Dad!"

"I'm divorced from your dad," she corrected calmly. "I've explained that over and over, Taylor."

"Some day he might come back."

"Even if he did, we're not married anymore, and that means I can fall in love with someone else. But I'll always love you. *Nothing* can ever change that."

Taylor was silent for a moment. She glanced at him worriedly and caught a glimpse of Cole's headlights in her rearview mirror.

"I thought you liked Cole," she said.

"I do. But Dad's my dad."

"Honey, I know that. And I'm happy that you love him. But you know you can't count on him to act like a father. He moved far away from us."

She wanted to tell him the truth, felt the words come to the tip of her tongue, but protecting Taylor was a deeply rooted instinct. This was not the right time. "He loves you very much," she said firmly. "But sometimes a husband and wife fall out of love. That's what happened with your dad and me."

"I don't get it." Taylor leaned forward in his seat to study her. "You're a good cook. You always look really pretty, and you get mad if I don't do what you tell me, but you're not *always* yelling, like other moms. What didn't Dad like?"

She stopped at a red light, on the brink of tears at his simple and surprising support. "People don't stop growing even when they become adults," she said. "They might not get any taller, but everybody's character keeps growing, and sometimes a husband and wife grow in different directions and want different things. Your dad and I didn't want the same things anymore."

"What did he want?"

"He wanted to be rich." The light changed and she

drove on. "And that's not a bad thing. Most people would like to be rich and have a nice house and a fancy car. But underneath all that, most people know that the really important things in life are having someone who loves you, having a job that you like, and enough money for food and a little bit of fun. And of course friends. When you appreciate those things, you're never unhappy, even if you don't have a lot of money."

"Dad was happy," Taylor argued. "Except just before he went away."

Danny had been a buddy to Taylor when things were going well. And even when they weren't, he never let Taylor see his dark, desperate moods. Until the last time…

"I'm just worried," Taylor said, his voice tight. "If Dad comes back, and Cole's with you, maybe he won't stay."

Worn down by the argument, Kara took the coward's way out. "I don't think that would happen, sweetie. But, anyway, all I did was kiss Cole. A lot more has to happen before a man and a woman decide they love each other and want to get married. So there's no need to worry at this point."

"But he likes you, too. I can tell."

"And I like him a lot because he likes you."

Taylor sighed. "It's kind of a mixed-up thing."

She glanced back at him. "That's life in a nutshell, sweetie."

CHAPTER EIGHT

COLE HAD TO ADMIT that the tree was spectacular. They'd placed it in Kara's old fluted Christmas tree stand, smack in front of the French doors. As Cole lay on his stomach under the tree to tighten the stand, branches in his ears and eyes, it did occur to him that there was something to be said for artificial trees that could be assembled branch by branch.

Mel crawled on his belly under the tree and licked Cole's face in support.

"That's perfect!" Kara cried, kicking lightly at the sole of Cole's shoe. "Come and look. Taylor, isn't it perfect?"

"Yeah," Taylor replied halfheartedly.

Cole crawled out and stood beside Kara. The tree was beautiful—tall, with evenly spaced branches—and already filling the room with fragrance. Mel barked his approval.

Kara beamed. Taylor had somehow reverted to the boy Cole had met the day he'd rescued Kara. Taylor had scarcely spoken since he'd arrived with Kara, and seemed determined to stay out of Cole's way. He couldn't imagine what accounted for the change in attitude. They'd had such a good time yesterday....

And then Cole had kissed Kara. Could that be what was bothering him?

"Looks good," Cole said.

"Good?" Kara challenged. "It's a wonderful tree. And wait until we get it decorated. Did you buy lights and garland?"

"I did."

"Do you have a ladder?"

He retrieved it from the garage and was carrying it toward the tree when the doorbell rang.

"Taylor, you want to get that?" Cole asked.

The boy ran to the door, Mel at his heels. Taylor reappeared with Blaine Hobson. Blaine was redheaded and freckled and wore wire-rimmed glasses. In one hand he carried a foil-wrapped plate.

"Mom sent cookies," he said, then he stared open-mouthed at the tree. "Wow! When'd you get that?"

"Last night. You like it?"

"You never have a tree."

"Well, Taylor thought I should have one," Cole explained. "Guys, this is Blaine Hobson from next door. He goes to St. Patrick's. Blaine, this is Taylor. And his mom, Mrs. Abbott."

Blaine nodded politely at Kara, then at Taylor. "A couple of my friends go to Courage Bay."

"I've only been there a year," Taylor said.

"Our soccer team plays yours. Are you on the team?"

Taylor stroked Mel's head, looking uncomfortable. "No. I have trouble kicking the ball. I'm not very good at running, either."

Blaine smiled widely. "Same. But I like to watch the games."

"Blaine can play chess and poker," Cole said, pulling the wrapper off a box of lights, "and he fixed my digital alarm clock. I thought it was broken, but it was just in the wrong mode. You guys want to help me put the lights on the tree?"

Kara assumed an authoritative stance near the ladder. "I'll supervise," she said, as the boys rushed to lend their assistance. She caught Cole's eye and winked as he climbed up.

"Good thing you brought lunch," he said, "or I'd accuse you of being a slacker."

"I'm saving myself for the fine work of stringing garlands and placing ornaments."

"Mom always has to take the lights off a couple of times before she gets them up right," Taylor said, as Cole placed one end of a string of lights in Taylor's hands. "Mom never swears, but she grumbles under her breath a lot."

"When I serve the lunch I brought," Kara said, "you'll be happy I'm here. How many boxes of lights did you buy?"

"Four." He secured the end of the string on a branch, then strung the lights around the tree with the boys' help.

"That might do," Kara said. "No, Cole. Closer than that."

"Mom likes *lots* of lights," Taylor said. "We have six strings, but our tree's bigger."

"Bigger than eight feet?" Cole asked in disbelief.

"We have eleven-foot ceilings." Kara walked around the tree, standing on tiptoe to adjust a row of lights. "Anything smaller than nine or ten feet disappears."

Cole seriously doubted that, but she seemed sincere.

"We have Mr. and Mrs. Santa in the porch swing," Taylor said, clearly happy about that. Then he frowned slightly. "And we're supposed to have reindeer on the roof, but we can't get them up there."

"Really?" Cole pretended surprise. "I thought they flew."

Taylor and Blaine looked at each other in confused concern. Then Taylor laughed. "No, you didn't! They're not real, anyway. They're just plastic."

"Oh. No wonder. Then I guess I'll have to come to your house and help you get them up."

"It's a steep roof," Kara warned.

Cole peered down at her from the ladder. "I got you down from the top of a tree at the top of a very high hill, remember?"

Her eyes locked with his for a moment, and he wondered if she was remembering the kiss. He certainly was.

"You had a friend with climbing gear," she reminded him.

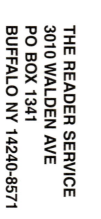

"Those were special circumstances," he countered. "A rooftop will seem like a piece of cake."

"Cool!" Taylor said. "I could help you. You can get onto the roof from my window."

Kara turned to him in sudden alarm. "You don't do that, do you?"

Taylor's eyes widened, and he reassured her quickly, "No. But Cole could."

Kara looked relieved. Cole couldn't believe she'd bought her son's denial. It was clear to him from Taylor's expression that the boy climbed onto the roof—probably often.

"That's all the lights, Mom," Taylor said. "What do you think?"

It was only too obvious to Cole that Taylor was trying to divert his mother's attention. And he did.

Kara examined the tree closely and nodded. "Looks good." She turned to Cole with a reluctant wince. "What kind of garland did you buy?" she asked. "That fuzzy foil stuff?"

He'd seen the thick foil ropes but had opted for a more natural-looking garland of bright red berries and pinecones. As he pulled the garland out of a bag and held it toward her, he teased, "Somehow I figured garland was an indicator of style. So there. I may have a smaller tree than yours, but it's going to be chic."

She smiled as she reached out to touch the realistic berries. "That's the garland I wanted to get for the mantel, but I couldn't afford it. It cost a fortune."

"I knew you'd be judging me on it, so I paid the price." He climbed the ladder, still looking superior. "All the way to the top?"

"No. Just a little way down so we can space the strands out. If the tree was against a wall, we could just do the front, but since it's going to be seen through the French doors, the back has to look as good as the front."

"You mean I should have bought more?"

"We can alternate it with some twiggy-looking stuff I didn't use this year. It'll add to the country air."

"Country air," he repeated, then said firmly, "No bows or lacy stuff."

"Well, of course not. Give me some credit."

"Country means bows and lace."

"In some circles. In mine it means natural stuff, old wood, old fabrics, dried flowers and greens."

There was a knock at the front door and Taylor raced over and peeked through a window to see who it was. "It's your aunt Shirley!" he reported, going to the door and pulling it open. "Hi!" he said as Shirley stepped inside. "We're putting up Cole's tree."

Shirley stopped in the middle of the living room to stare at the tree, clearly incredulous. "Oh my." She put a hand to her heart. "I may have to sit down."

Kara had crawled under the tree to plug in the lights, and even with just the garland strung, it was beautiful.

"Hi, Aunt Shirley." Cole turned to Taylor and Blaine. "Taylor, you take Aunt Shirley's coat, and

Blaine, you can get her a cup of coffee, please. The coffee's in the kitchen—just call if you need help."

The boys scurried to do his bidding as Kara scooted out backward from under the tree, presenting a delicious view.

"How tall is it?" Shirley asked.

Kara went to an overstuffed chair and fluffed the pillow in it, then motioned for his aunt to sit. "Eight feet. We're very proud of that, considering Cole originally wanted a tree that would stand on a table."

Shirley studied her for a moment, then turned her gaze back to the tree. "As I live and breathe," she said. "Last year he bought lots of presents, but otherwise, there wasn't a sign of Christmas in this house."

"I'm usually at work," Cole protested, "and we spent Christmas day at your house." Although Cole believed in the spirit of Christmas, he had no use for the trappings. When he was first married he'd made an effort, but Angela had always been on the road, and putting up a tree had only reminded him that he didn't have anyone to share it with.

"When you do come home," Kara said, gently resting her hand on his sleeve, "you'll be surprised how much this touches you, revitalizes you."

It touched him already. He just wasn't sure how good that was in the long run. He really didn't need to resurrect the longing for all the things he'd decided it was easier to live without.

The feel of her hand on his arm was causing a powerful reaction in him. Anytime he came in contact with Kara, he seemed to undergo a molecular change.

As if aware of that reaction, she drew away and smiled at Shirley as Blaine brought Cole's aunt a cup of coffee. Blaine had spent enough time at Cole's to know how she liked it.

"I brought coffee cake," Kara said, heading for the kitchen. "Shall we all take a break?"

KARA LIKED THE WAY Cole teased his aunt unmercifully about the designer sweatsuit she wore. The way he poured her more coffee, then went to his garage to get the vacuum cleaner he'd fixed for her, and put it in the trunk of her car.

"He's such a honey," Shirley said to Kara when he carried the vacuum cleaner out, the boys and the dog determined to help him whether he needed them or not. She patted Kara's hand on the table. "So, how serious is this?"

"Not serious at all," Kara fibbed, afraid of shocking the woman with the intensity of her feelings. "We're just helping him put up his tree."

Shirley leaned toward her conspiratorially. "I think it's more serious than you realize."

Unable to lie to Cole's aunt, Kara decided to confide in her. "I'd be happy with that, but I know Cole's concerned about what went wrong with his first marriage."

"Whatever went wrong," Shirley replied, glancing

toward the door, "was with Angela. Cole was hardworking, faithful—gave her all the flexibility her work on the road required, even when it afforded him none of the things he wanted in a marriage." She shrugged. "I was living in Portland then, but Brad told me all about it. Angela was a nice enough girl, but she was never as committed to her marriage as she was to her career."

Cole and the boys burst back into the room, still laughing, and the time for confidences was over.

Shirley opened a small round hatbox she'd brought in with her and handed it to Cole. "I must say my timing is perfect. Although, I thought you'd want to take these to work to share with your friends rather than use them yourself."

The boys leaned over Cole's shoulders and Kara went around the table to watch him lift out what looked like cookies. There were about a dozen in various shapes—hearts, stars, bells, wreaths—and each one had a cut-out center that resembled colored glass.

"They're called stained glass cookies," Shirley said, confirming Kara's thoughts. "The glass is fruit glaze. But don't try to eat them, because I sealed them with hair spray. They'll look beautiful on your tree, Cole."

The boys hurried to hang them up. When the lights caught the sparkling "glass," the ornaments gleamed.

Cole gave his aunt a hug. "Thanks, Aunt," he said with sincere affection. "I love them."

A short time later, Shirley got up to say her goodbyes.

"Stay for lunch," Cole suggested. "Kara brought something."

"Spaghetti casserole," Kara said. "Fruit salad and bread sticks. Taylor's favorite things."

Shirley made an appreciative sound. "I'd love to, but the grannies and I are due at Candy's for a work party. We have a booth at the annual Christmas fair, and we're taking all our crafts over to see if we have enough."

"I hope you'll be selling those stained glass cookie ornaments," Kara said, helping her with her coat.

"We will—" Shirley hooked her arm in Kara's as they walked to the door.

Cole noted the gesture and raised an eyebrow.

"But I'll leave some for you with Cole."

"No, I want to buy them."

"But I want to give them to you, and you have to do what I say because I'm older," Shirley said firmly.

Kara looked at her dubiously. "Who made that rule?"

"I did. Cole knows all about it. He'll tell you it's pointless to argue with me." She hugged Kara, then Cole, then each of the boys.

They all walked out with her, and minutes later waved her off as she peeled away with a loud and slightly erratic burst of speed.

"You're lucky to have her," Kara said as they trooped back inside. "My mother was always so full of her own problems. It's hard to have to bottle up all the little things you really want to share with someone."

"I miss my dad a lot, too," Taylor said. "We didn't talk much, but I liked being with him."

No matter how many times Kara heard her son say he missed his father, the guilt she felt never lessened.

Cole nodded. "I know. I missed my dad for a long time, even though I knew he left because he didn't want to be with us."

Kara saw that Taylor was struggling with Cole's words. He was telling himself that his father left because he didn't want to be with Kara, not because he didn't want to be with Taylor. She squared her shoulders. It was better for Taylor to believe that than to know the truth: his father had walked away from both of them because he was a common criminal and never gave a thought to either of them.

"My dad got a divorce so he could join the army," Taylor told Blaine.

Blaine frowned. "You don't need a divorce to do that."

Kara stepped forward quickly, encouraging the boys to open the box of ornaments she'd brought. "Put the bigger ones on the bottom," she directed, ignoring Cole's questioning glance, "and Cole will climb the ladder to put the smaller ones on the top."

"At home, we have a star for the top of the tree," Blaine said, "and when you plug it in, it sparkles!"

Taylor turned to Cole worriedly. "Did you buy something for the top?"

"No," he replied. "Can't I just leave it?"

Taylor put both hands to his face. "No! There *has* to be something at the top of the tree. We have an angel. Some people have a star or this funny tall ornament thing, but there has to be *something*."

"Okay, I'll find something."

"It has to be special," Taylor explained. "Ours was Mom's when she was a little girl. And before that it was her grandma's."

"Well…special things have to start somewhere," Cole said, carrying the box of ornaments to the tree. "So even if I do have to buy it, it'll be special because you told me I had to get it. And I'll let you put it up for me."

Taylor turned to Kara. "Is that okay?"

"Sure," she replied, touched and suddenly a little worried. What if Cole's involvement in this relationship wasn't as serious as Shirley thought? What if he liked her son because he could relate to how much Taylor missed his dad, but didn't particularly care about her? Was that even a consideration after their kiss? Was she just torturing herself, as she had a tendency to do?

She worried all the way through lunch while Cole and the boys talked about police work while devouring her casserole and salad. Taylor and Blaine finally ran outside with Mel to let off steam, and Cole helped himself to the last spoonful of casserole.

"This is delicious," he said, sprinkling Parmesan on it. "I'm surprised you didn't become a chef with your talent in the kitchen."

She shrugged. "I've always loved to cook, but I'm passionate about music."

He nodded thoughtfully. "Angela was like that. And she wasn't happy unless she was sharing it with an audience."

"In my case," she said, "the passion's deep, but the talent isn't. I love sharing with children, because they think my meager talents are good enough, and I do the absolute best I can for them."

"Is Taylor showing any musical tendencies?"

She leaned her chin on her hand and watched her son through the French doors. He and Blaine seemed to enjoy each other's company. She was happy about that. "Oh, he likes to sing along with CDs. And he helped me pick out carols for my group's Christmas gig. But he's more interested in his science class and flatly refuses to play a musical instrument."

"All kids resist the family business, so to speak—don't they?"

She looked away, feeling wistful as she thought of the close relationship she and Taylor used to share. "I think mostly he's resisting me. I know he loves me, but from his point of view, the divorce is all my fault. Uprooting him so I could take this job hasn't helped."

COLE THOUGHT TWICE about his response, but decided not to hold back. He'd been watching Kara with Taylor all morning, and he saw something worrisome in her behavior. "Are you sure telling him his father joined the military was a good move?"

She sat up, instantly defensive. He'd figured that would be her reaction. But she was becoming important to him, and he thought the subject worth exploring.

"I'm never sure of anything. But I want Taylor to be certain that both his parents love him, even though they aren't together." Her snapping eyes and set chin told him she didn't want to discuss the subject further.

But he'd gone this far, and he remembered how close he and his mother and brother had become as they'd worked together to adjust to his father's defection.

"To make him a hero, though, when he's really responsible for all the—"

"Little boys need heroes," she interrupted.

"Little boys need to know they're being dealt with honestly. That no matter how hard things get, they can depend on somebody for the truth."

She went pale. "You wouldn't tell him?"

He couldn't believe she would ask that. "Of course I wouldn't tell him. But I think *you* should."

"He's upset enough that his father's gone. Thinking he's doing heroic things rather than wasting his days in jail gives him something to be proud of, rather than embarrassed about."

"Are you embarrassed that *you* loved him?" he asked, guessing he was only getting himself into deeper trouble. But he thought he'd detected something of her own humiliation in that remark. He hadn't known Kara long, but she always seemed so together, so in charge, and he figured it might be good for her to admit that the past few years had been difficult.

He was right about her reaction. She straightened in her chair and became cool, putting him at a distance.

"I'm embarrassed that my love meant so little to him, that his time with his son was so expendable, and that he was willing to throw it all away in the interest of getting rich quickly."

He leaned toward her, not wanting her to shut him out. "So you misread him," he said, "or he changed. That can happen. You thought he was more of a man than he turned out to be. If anyone should be embarrassed, shouldn't it be him?"

She put her fork down and reached for her coffee. "Maybe. It doesn't matter now."

"It does matter," he insisted. "You're making an idol out of him for Taylor's sake, and that isn't right. He'll feel betrayed by you when he finds out. You have to see things as they are and then move on."

"No, that's *your* M.O." She banged her cup on the table. Coffee sloshed out and she mopped it up with her napkin. "You want to get your marriage all figured out, but the truth is, you can't. How can you hope to know what went wrong when you had a false impression of the person you married in the first place? From what you've said, Angela changed on you just like Danny changed on me.

"And if you can't get it straight, then you don't *have* to move on, and that saves you from having to get it right the next time, because you never try for a next time. And all for seemingly noble reasons." She pushed back from the table and got to her feet. "I'm on to you, Winslow, so don't try to analyze *me*. I think the great paragon who can protect and serve everyone else is doing his best to protect himself as well."

That hurt, as he was sure she'd intended, and it was instinctive to want to hurt her in return. "At least I'm not lying to my child," he shot back.

"No," she retorted, "you're just lying to *yourself*." She grabbed her jacket from the back of the chair. "Good luck, Cole. Just return my stuff after the holidays."

Kara went to the French doors to call Taylor, but the backyard was empty. Mel and the boys were in Blaine's backyard playing in a makeshift fort. She called Taylor's name, but the boys were laughing so hard, he didn't hear her. Turning, she headed for the front door.

Cole caught her arm. There'd been no satisfaction in hurting her, and he hated what had happened to their day together. "So, that's it? You don't want to fight it out?"

She stood stiffly in his grasp. "What's the point? You told me up front you have no intention of remarrying, and we disagree on how I'm raising Taylor, so there'd be little point in getting to know each other any better. It doesn't seem anything could come of it."

"I think you're doing a great job with Taylor," he corrected, tightening his grip as she tried to pull free. "I just don't think you should sacrifice your relationship with him to pump up your husband. He doesn't deserve Taylor's admiration anyway. I don't see why you can't make the point that it's all right for Taylor to love his dad, even though he's a louse."

"It's trickier than that." She rolled her eyes. "But how would you know? You've never had children."

He refused to flinch. "I didn't mean to be intrusive," he said, still holding her. "I just hate to see you hurt."

"Please don't concern yourself with my feelings. I'm very resilient. Just let go of my arm and I'll get out of your comfortable bachelor space."

"Look, I know I've hurt you, but we need to argue this through. You're the one running away."

Suddenly, she slumped, and all the passion and temper of a moment ago vanished. That made Cole feel even worse.

"To tell you the truth," she said on a sigh, "I was attracted to you, but now I'm beginning to remember how much I hated having someone second-guessing me—or trying to figure out what on earth I seem to be lacking. You don't have the heart for a relationship anyway, Cole, and that's killed the attraction."

Okay, now she was going over the line. "Really."

"You tell yourself you need to know what went wrong with your marriage, when actually you just need to be safe."

She spoke the words with complete conviction, and the only way he could think to dispute them was to take action in the most dangerous way he could imagine. So he kissed her right there in the middle of the living room, slipping his hand up the back of her sweater and splaying his fingers against her back. It felt warm and fragile against his palm.

For just an instant she resisted, then she leaned into him, coming alive with a fire that belied her earlier denial of attraction to him.

With a bang, the front door burst open, and before they could draw apart, Taylor, Blaine and Mel had surrounded them.

"Mom," Taylor said, his eyebrows practically disappearing into his hair. "Why are you hanging from Cole's neck?"

Cole couldn't wait to hear her answer to that one.

CHAPTER NINE

KARA WAS HOT from head to toe. Her cheeks flamed, her ears burned, the tips of her breasts were tight, and her feet felt as though they dangled above the fires of hell. She hadn't even realized she was "hanging from Cole's neck," as her son had so bluntly phrased it.

Cole set her on her feet and she avoided his eyes as she turned to her son, pretending to be quite at ease with what he'd seen. "Mistletoe goes up next," she said. "We were just practicing."

Taylor looked doubtful. "Where is it?"

"Uh..." Instinctively, she glanced up, but all she could see was a light fixture and fan.

"In the refrigerator," Cole replied gamely. "Aunt Shirley brought some and told me to keep it in there until I put it up."

Taylor frowned, apparently still undecided about whether he believed them. "It's gotta be up before you start kissing people."

"It can be anywhere," Blaine corrected. "It even works if you hold it over your head."

"But it's in the fridge," Taylor argued.

"I don't have a hook for it yet," Cole said. "We couldn't very well stand in the fridge to try it out."

He turned his back on the boys and grinned at Kara with a wickedness that made her cheeks feel even warmer.

"Nice to know it works, though. Let me get your bowl for you," he said.

"We're leaving?" Taylor complained. "How come? The tree isn't all up! Is Cole coming home with us to put up the reindeer? Blaine was gonna show me his Air Athletes battle station!"

"I have some things to do for class tomorrow," Kara told him. She got his jacket and helped him into it. When he resisted, she put one of his arms in a sleeve. "Cole can finish the tree himself, and he has things to do, too. We'll figure out how to put up the reindeer. Blaine can come home with us, if it's okay with his mom."

Taylor was momentarily torn between happiness at her suggestion and disappointment at having to leave. "Mo-om," he whined.

Kara was surprised that having a friend over didn't compensate for leaving a little early. Cole Winslow was powerful stuff.

"I thought we were gonna be here all day," Taylor grumbled. "I thought we were gonna finish the tree. Blaine's mom said he could stay and help till it was done."

"I...miscalculated," Kara said lamely. "I forgot I

had to print up carol books for tomorrow. We have our first gig after lunch."

"I bet you're just making that up." Taylor folded his arms in a pout. He looked accusingly at Cole. "Did you say something to make her mad?"

"I think I might have," Cole said, handing Kara the bowl and glancing her way with an accusing frown of his own. He put a hand on the shoulder of each boy and walked them to the door. "I'll be more careful next time. And I'll be over to put up the reindeer. Blaine, go ask your mom if you can go with Taylor and Mrs. Abbott. Tell her I can vouch for them."

Blaine and Taylor ran off together.

"I've got a ladder. I'll handle the reindeer." Kara managed to sound firm as she stepped outside, but she'd lost her angry steam the moment he'd pulled her into his arms. She could still feel his strong, warm hands on her back, and she shivered involuntarily. "Thank you for your hospitality," she said with cool politeness, but her voice was raspy.

"You're welcome," he replied, sounding amused at the discomfort she was trying so hard to hide. "Thank you for the kiss."

"I didn't give it. You took it."

"Kara, be honest," he chided gently.

"Okay," she agreed reluctantly. "I was a willing participant. And I enjoyed it. But I already admitted I'm attracted to you."

"I'm flattered," he said as he walked her to the car,

"because I'm wild about you. And please don't accuse me of not having the heart for a relationship, when all I want to do is make sure we know what we're doing."

Kara unlocked the passenger door and yanked it open. Just once she'd like a man to be so wild about her that he threw caution to the wind and risked everything for her.

But then, that was how Danny operated. Not with her, of course, but his reckless action seldom had a good outcome.

So, what *did* she want?

She had to admit she didn't know. Her brain was a muddle of hopeful expectations and scary memories.

"What are you thinking about?" he asked. "You look grumpy."

She forced a smile when the boys came running out of Blaine's house, talking and laughing. A pretty red-haired woman in green slacks and a green-and-beige sweater followed them. She looked like a model in a Ralph Lauren ad.

"Hi!" she said warmly, hand extended as she walked around the car toward Kara. "I'm Cindy Hobson. Blaine says you've invited him over. Hi, Cole."

Kara shook hands, explaining that she and Taylor had come to help Cole put up his tree, but now she had to go home to prepare for her choir's first paying concert. She purposely avoided looking at Cole.

"But Cole never has a tree." Cindy sounded shocked.

"So I've heard, but we thought he should."

"I see. Well, if you're sure Blaine won't be in your way."

"I'm sure. And I'll bring him home after dinner, if that's okay with you."

"Sounds perfect. My husband's golfing, so while he and Blaine are both gone, I can get their presents wrapped. I'd be happy to return the favor for you some evening."

"I may just take you up on that," Kara told her. "I'll have Blaine back by seven-thirty."

"Be good, honey," Cindy cautioned her son as he and Taylor scrambled into the car. "Help with the dishes." She blew Blaine a kiss, then started back to the house. Halfway up the walk, she turned to grin at Cole. "A tree, huh? No grinch this year?"

"I'm never a grinch," Cole said, pretending she'd hurt his feelings.

"Scrooge, then."

"*'Bye*, Cindy."

She laughed. "'Bye, Cole," she called as she hurried up the walk.

"It's amazing," Cole said, opening Kara's door for her, "that a simple Christmas tree is the source of so much speculation."

"That's because Christmas trees aren't simple," Kara told him. "They're a symbol of the season and a mirror of your personality."

"But you and Taylor decorated my tree."

"Aunt Shirley provided the stained glass cookies. Christmas trees can also reflect the people in our lives."

He held the door as she climbed inside.

She needed desperately to leave. This conversation was leading places she didn't want to go. And the fact that Cole looked as though he didn't want her to leave made her hurry. "Don't forget to get a tree-topper," she reminded him, then tugged the door out of his hands. She was a little disappointed that he let her go so easily.

KARA WAS SURPRISED to find Loren Ford pulling out of her driveway as she drove up. She parked on the street, but he stopped at the end of her drive and got out. Kara climbed out, too, wondering if something had gone wrong at the school.

"We're going to go inside, Mom," Taylor said. He and Blaine ran toward the house, making motor noises.

As Kara approached Loren, he reached into his open window and withdrew a pink poinsettia and a box of chocolates. He held them out to her.

"Hi!" he said cheerfully. "I thought I'd try one more time to see if you'll change your mind about coming with me to the Christmas Ball."

"Uh…"

"I thought the pink poinsettia was more you," Loren said when she hesitated. "And the chocolates are Belgian—the best I could find."

"Loren, that's so thoughtful." After Cole's criticism

of her parenting skills and her complete confusion about their relationship, flowers and candy were a welcome expression of affection.

"I'd love to go to the ball with you," she said impulsively. Loren knew she regarded him as her boss and a friend. Besides, he'd be far easier on her heart than Cole.

Loren appeared momentarily shocked, then he said, "Great! We'll have a wonderful time. Dinner first?"

"That would be nice."

"I'll pick you up at seven-thirty." He left quickly, probably afraid she'd change her mind.

She returned his wave and pulled her car into the driveway. Almost immediately she began to second guess her decision.

But she shook off her doubt. It was just a dance, and her social life sure needed a boost.

AT 1:00 A.M., Cole sat on his living room floor, Mel beside him. All the lights were off except for those on the Christmas tree, and the colorful glow, reflected in the French doors, seemed to cast a magical spell. He tried to imagine how Kara would set the sight to music—Chopin, perhaps. Or maybe, more appropriately, a Christmas carol.

On the coffee table was an angel he'd bought after Kara had left with the boys. He'd intended to find a star for the top of the tree—the angel seemed too feminine for his house—but then he'd spotted this traditional angel with a banner stretched between her arms. It read Love, and musical notes were scattered across it. The music theme had reminded him of Kara, and it had no longer mattered if the angel was feminine or not. She was perfect.

"Special," as Taylor had said.

Mel gave a low rumble, apparently in agreement.

Cole felt a moment's trepidation as he realized that his feelings for Kara Abbott had become serious so fast. Any attempt to keep his distance was out of the question. Just thinking about her as he stared up at the tree she'd helped create made his pulse race. He chose to ignore the fact that she was mad at him.

But he couldn't forget there was a child involved. Taylor had enough pain in his life. Cole didn't want to add to it, which he would do if things went bad.

Still, he hadn't felt this hopeful in a long time. So filled with...joy. He could just imagine what his buddies at the station would say if they heard that one. *Joy.* In his mind, he saw another angel holding a banner with the simple three-letter word.

"WOW." BRAD STOOD in the middle of Cole's living room the following morning, staring at the Christmas tree. "You never have a tree, and yet here I am, standing in front of...an honest-to-God Christmas tree."

Cole had been trying to get his brother out the door for the past five minutes. But Brad continued to stare at the tree.

"Get over it, will you," Cole said, grabbing his arm and pushing him toward the door. "It's just a tree."

It wasn't, of course. Cole knew that. He'd been awake most of the night dealing with what it meant—and all the problems it presented.

"This is all because of that pretty little bird you plucked out of the trees, isn't it. Hey! Don't shove!"

"Then move it, will you? And let's take your truck, since you're parked behind me. We've got two hours until your shift starts, and Emily let me have you on the promise that I'd baby-sit this weekend so the two of you could go out to dinner. So you'd better do your part here."

"Brad Junior's a pleasure to spend time with. You'll enjoy it."

Cole had visions of the baby crying and his not knowing what to do, of diapers he wouldn't know how to change. He wasn't looking forward to baby-sitting, but he did have to get to know his nephew.

"Where are we going, anyway?" Brad asked, fastening his seat belt. "You asked for help with your roof."

"Not my roof."

"Whose roof?"

"Kara's roof."

"Ah." Brad kept a straight face, but Cole knew he was holding back a smirk. "Loose shingles?"

"No."

"Birds in the chimney?"

"No."

At Cole's direction, Brad turned onto the road that led the short distance to Kara's.

Brad glanced his way in puzzlement. "I've run out of guesses."

"Reindeer," Cole replied tersely.

"I see." Brad sounded smug.

"We're going to put them up."

"Well, I hope they don't struggle, because if I arrive at the hospital with hoofprints on my face..."

"Someday I'm going to hit you so hard..." Cole threatened.

"You've been promising that for thirty years."

"I'm closer to doing it than I've ever been."

"Santa wouldn't like it."

"Santa isn't here."

"If we're putting his reindeer on a rooftop, he'll be along, I assure you."

Cole pointed out Kara's driveway. In the middle of the morning, the house and the neighborhood were quiet. He was hoping the reindeer would be in the garage. Taylor had said Kara had taken them down from a high shelf, but decided they were too heavy to try to put up herself.

When Cole tried the garage door, it was locked. He walked around it, found a small, high window and saw that the old-fashioned twist lock was open.

"Does Kara know you're going to do this?" Brad asked suspiciously as Cole beckoned him to the window.

"We talked about it, then we argued. I thought I'd put them up to surprise her."

Brad folded his arms over his chest. "We're going to put decorations on a roof and you didn't bring a ladder?"

"Kara's got one in the garage."

"This is breaking and entering."

"Don't tell me the law. This is…raising and entering."

"If we end up in the slammer…"

"The neighborhood's quiet as a tomb. There's no one around to call the police. And Kara wouldn't press charges anyway."

"I thought you said you argued."

"Don't you and Emily argue?"

"Occasionally, but we're married."

"Enough of this conversation," Cole said. "Now, give me a boost up."

Brad locked his hands together and Cole stepped up to grab the sill. As soon as Cole had raised the window, Brad let go.

"Hey!" Cole yelled, clinging to the sill.

Somehow he managed to gain purchase with his feet against the side of the garage. Swinging one leg over, he climbed through the window and came down on an old door laid flat between a sink and an old stove. It must have been used as a shelf or table. A string dangled in his face and he reached up to pull it. Light from a bare bulb illuminated the old garage.

He spotted the reindeer instantly. They were made of plastic and trimmed in lights. If there'd been a full team of nine to begin with, there were now only four, their front legs drawn up in flight. Rudolph remained in the lead, however, a large red bulb for his nose.

Cole searched for a ladder. Kara had said she had one. He spotted it hanging sideways on hooks on the wall. To reach it, he had to pull a stack of boxes out of a dark corner. The ladder was halfway down when Cole felt something sharp stab the middle of his back. With a clatter, the ladder fell onto the pile of boxes.

"Don't...move," a deep, trembling voice said forcefully, "or you'll spend the rest of your life in several pieces."

Had he gotten the wrong house? Cole wondered, and started to turn around.

"I said don't move!" the deep voice repeated, and Cole felt the sharp object push painfully against his spine. In the same instant, he recognized the voice.

Before he could say anything, shouts and a weird thumping noise sounded outside.

"I've got him!" Kara shouted toward the open window. "Did you call 911?"

More shouting and thumping came through the window.

"Kara, it's me," Cole said, taking his life in his hands and turning. Brad was apparently getting the bad end of something out there, and if Cole was going to save him, he had to move now. "Call off whoever's out there beating up my brother. We came to put up your reindeer."

Kara, in a green woolen dress and Christmas-wreath earrings, her hair long and loose and falling around her face in soft waves, stared at him first in shock, then in mounting dismay.

Cole wasn't doing much better. It was hard for a seasoned cop to realize he'd been held captive by a woman with a butter knife.

He took the weapon from her, and to cover his own embarrassment, demanded, "What are you *doing*?"

"What are *you* doing?" Kara gasped. "My neighbor called to tell me someone was climbing through my garage window."

"You came to investigate with a *butter* knife? Where's your car, anyway? And why aren't you at school?"

She blinked, as though unsure which question to deal with first. "Christmas vacation started today. Jared's mother dropped me off to pick up a change of clothes. We're going to set up a booth... Hey, wait a minute!" Temper ignited her eyes. "Where's *your* truck? I heard noises, looked out and saw a completely strange vehicle. I figured someone knew I was gone all day and was about to steal from me!"

It was all he could do not to shake her. "If you hear a strange noise and suspect you're being robbed, the correct response is to call the police, then go to a neighbor's. You don't arm yourself with a butter knife and try to make an arrest."

"Well, pardon me for being unfamiliar with proper intruder-handling etiquette! I didn't want you to get away!"

He knew she didn't mean that last remark quite the way he might have liked her to, but the words struck home anyway. "I'm not going anywhere," he said, feeling his blood pressure lower.

Apparently Kara was calmer, too. "What *are* you doing in my garage?" she asked.

"I told you—I came to put up your reindeer."

"You could have warned me."

"I wanted to surprise you."

They looked into each other's eyes, and at the same moment realized that's exactly what he'd done. Both of them started to laugh, until a very loud shout caught their attention.

"Oh my God!" Kara said, running to the garage door. "Mrs. McGinley called to tell me she saw someone climbing through my garage window. I asked her to phone the police."

Oh, great. The guys at the department were going to love this.

Cole helped her raise the garage door. There stood Brad between two uniformed officers, each holding one of his arms. His hair was disheveled, and there were tiny scratch marks on his face. Beside them stood a woman in black bike pants and a gold lamé shirt. Her bright red hair was tied up in a gold scarf, and she wore large-framed glasses and dangling rhinestone earrings.

She pointed at Cole with a hearth broom that boasted a red-and-green bow and had been decorated with berry boughs.

"That's him!" she said. "Climbed in through the garage window with the help of this one." She pointed the broom at Brad, as though she would have swept him away with the soot.

Cole guessed the shouts and thumps he'd heard through the garage window had been Brad on the receiving end of the broom.

The woman pointed to Cole again. "This is thieving of the worst kind. A Christmas crook!"

"Winslow!" It was Officer George Mendez, a portly, middle-aged man Cole had ridden with a few times.

"Cole!" Officer Miranda Charpentier said at the same time. She was blond and fulsome, the close-fitting uniform enhancing her considerable attributes. "What are you doing?"

Miranda and Cole had dated a couple of times. She was happy with a casual relationship and assured Cole she was as determined to remain single as he was. Then she'd asked him if he'd ever thought about having children, and he'd never called her again. She'd taken the breakup in stride, though she'd teased him about being super-sensitive on the issue of marriage. Her eyes now held a familiar warmth as she waited for his answer.

"This is Kara Abbott," he said. "She's a friend of mine. I promised to put up her reindeer."

Mrs. McGinley curled her lip at Cole as though he was the lowest of life forms. "Probably planned to steal all her possessions, then lie in wait to rape and murder her, too."

Brad groaned. "Yeah, that sounds like us. Mendez, we were just raising and entering." Brad knew Mendez from the E.R. Police officers often accompanied victims of crimes and suspects.

"Pardon me?" Mendez said.

Cole sent Brad a quelling look. "Kara will explain. Won't you, Kara?"

"If this woman is a friend of yours," Charpentier asked, giving Kara a vaguely disdainful look, "why don't you have a key to the place?"

"Because he's not that kind of friend," Kara said, returning the same look. "Everything's fine, Officers. I'm sorry we bothered you at a time when you're probably very busy."

Mendez smiled. "Not a problem. You watch yourself with these two reprobates here, Mrs. Abbott."

"You never put up *my* reindeer," Charpentier said in an undertone to Cole, but still loud enough for Kara to hear. Even Brad and Mendez looked her way.

"There was probably no need to," Kara replied, her dark eyes studying Charpentier's unconsciously seductive hazel ones. "It's pretty clear you're on the naughty list."

Charpentier reacted to the softly spoken words like a cat arching its back. Then her eyes filled with reluctant respect and she, too, smiled. "You all have a good afternoon. And we don't want to come back here with a call that someone's fallen off the roof."

"We'll be careful," Kara promised. She hugged her neighbor. "And thanks for looking out for me, Mrs. McGinley."

Kara's genuine appreciation of the older woman's vigilance seemed to make up for Mrs. McGinley's disappointment at the lack of arrests.

The two police officers got back into their cruiser, and Mrs. McGinley went home.

Kara greeted Brad with a quick, tight smile, then focused on Cole. "I told you I could put up the reindeer myself."

"Sorry," Cole said. "But I knew Taylor wanted the reindeer on the roof and I had the time to do it."

That seemed to annoy her, though he couldn't imagine why. "And what have you done for Officer Charpentier?"

"Pardon me?" The non sequitur surprised him.

"The beautiful cop. You have a history?"

A tricky question. He could see the potential pitfalls in his answer, but there seemed no point in lying. "Yes, we have. It was brief, but it's a history." He was aware of Brad heading toward the garage.

She was silent for a moment, then drew a deep breath. "I know you're entitled to a history," she said, frowning at him. "I just wonder why you weren't afraid of doing it wrong with *her*?"

"It?"

"Life. A relationship."

"Because the only thing we did together," he replied significantly, "is hard to do wrong."

It was difficult to tell from her taut features whether she was upset by his words. Or whether she even really understood what he meant. "We were interested in creating a relationship that involved only—"

"I understand," she interrupted. "You used each other for sex. I'm just wondering why contact of any kind with her didn't frighten you away. I personally think she's very scary. And no matter what she told you, I'll bet she had marriage in mind all along. She has that possessive look."

"She did have marriage in mind. That's why we didn't last very long."

"Then you'd better forget the reindeer," she said, turning her back on him, "because that's what I have in mind, too."

He followed her into the garage. Brad passed them carrying the ladder Cole had dropped.

"I told you I was crazy about you."

She went through a small back door and across a patch of grass to the side door of her old farmhouse. Cole followed right behind her.

"That wouldn't be enough in the long run," she argued.

"It's a start."

Once inside the house, she stopped in the middle of

a large yellow-and-white kitchen. She turned on him, her eyes sparking, her body bristling. "You confuse me! You try to keep your distance, but you do very nice things for me, and you kiss me as though…"

"As though I'm crazy about you."

"As though I'm important to you, which is a very different thing. Your argument for caution makes sense—sort of—but is logic really what it's about? Danny hurt me, so I can put him behind me. Your wife hurt you, but you can't forget her." She shook her head, then sighed. "I'm sorry. Maybe your marriage had better moments than mine."

COLE TOOK KARA'S ARM and led her toward a small wicker love seat off to one side of her kitchen that formed a kind of sitting area. He encouraged her to take a seat, but she refused.

"What few people know, other than Brad and me," he said, his expression grim, "is that Angela was pregnant when she died."

That was the last thing Kara had expected to hear. She did sit down, and as she thought about what he'd said, she felt compassion for him, and a new respect. The whole issue of a relationship between them changed with these words.

He sat beside her. "An autopsy was conducted because there was another vehicle involved and they were trying to determine culpability. The driver was drinking…and Angela was pregnant." He paused, leaning a hand against the back of the love seat. "At first I thought it was somebody else's baby and that was why she was leaving me. Then I realized how far along she was, and that it was mine. She'd been home three months earlier for a few weeks, and I'd been determined to stabilize our marriage. She tried, too, I think, but it didn't work." He put a hand to his heart in a gesture of vulnerability that caused her as much pain as it seemed to cause him. "I lost a baby, and I feel a…a guilt, a sadness I can't seem to shake."

She didn't know what else to do. She put her arms around him to comfort him. "I'm sorry. I'm so sorry." A year after Taylor was born, Kara had miscarried. She understood his grief. "That's a terrible loss, and I apologize for pushing you. I didn't understand." She drew out of his arms, knowing the only thing she could do for this relationship right now was step back. Hadn't she decided that yesterday anyway? Why was she arguing with him?

She smiled up at him. "Please don't worry about the reindeer and just do what you need to do for Christmas."

"I need to help you get the reindeer up," he said, his gaze holding hers as though he read her mind. "And I need you to be part of my life. So don't look as though you're going to back away, because I won't let you."

She didn't know if she was strong enough to be part of his life. A warm, snugly holiday would be hard to live down in the light of a cold new year.

Cole stood abruptly. "Brad volunteered to help me and he goes on duty in about an hour. We wasted a lot of time, thanks to your neighbor."

She had to smile at that. Then she heard the tap of a horn outside and realized that Jared's mom was back. For a few minutes there, she'd almost forgotten that she had a life aside from the one that existed in the depths of Cole's eyes.

"I have to go," she said, gathering up the purse and jacket and the change of clothes she'd collected. "You sure you two are going to be all right up there?"

"I'm sure." He followed her to the door. She made a point of leaving it unlocked. "Just help yourselves if you need a cup of coffee or the bathroom." She smiled again. "I'll tell Mrs. McGinley it's okay."

"I'd appreciate that," he said with a grin.

In front of the house, they looked up at the roof. Brad was positioning Rudolph near the chimney.

"Thank you!" Kara shouted up at him.

He blew her a kiss, then pointed to the grass where the other reindeer lay. "Cole, send up another one!"

"Better get to work," Cole said, leaning down to give her a chaste kiss on the cheek. "You getting your Christmas shopping done this Saturday?"

"Yes." She waved at Cassie, Jared's mom, who watched with interest from inside the idling car.

"I'll come along and carry for you, but I have to work the Grannies' booth at the fair in the afternoon."

She was about to tell him that she was going to dinner and the ball with Loren that night, but something held her back.

Instead she said, "You don't have to…"

"I'd like to," he insisted.

"Okay. We're moving the wrapping booth from the mall to the fair in the afternoon."

"I'll pick you and Taylor up for breakfast?"

"Taylor, Finlay and Blaine are going to the Kiwanis Kids Christmas party at eight in the morning, then Cindy's making cookies with them in the afternoon."

"Who's Finlay?"

"Our neighbor. A very smart, very twenty-first-century young lady."

"Just you and me, then. Around eight o'clock?"

"Sure."

"Good. Go back to school. We'll have these reindeer ready to light up when you come home."

"Thank you."

"My pleasure."

As Kara climbed into Cassie's car, she knew her face reflected her dismay. Now that Cole had explained about his lost baby, she understood why he was so hesitant about trusting himself to fall in love again. The thought of spending an evening with Loren had suddenly become even less appealing.

CHAPTER TEN

KARA AND HER CHORUS caroled for days. They had a series of back-to-back gigs, several office Christmas parties and an invitation to sing at City Hall. She worked the gift-wrap booth at the mall every evening, where she was overwhelmed by the Christmas spirit.

Taylor was so alive with it he could hardly contain his energy. He and Blaine were together constantly now that school was out for the holidays. They usually stayed at Kara's, since she could be home with them. When she had to be away with the chorus, Cindy paid for both boys to attend a Christmas gifts workshop sponsored by one of the churches over the Christmas break.

This holiday warmth was what she'd always wanted as a child but never had. Her mother had been convinced that without money to buy gifts there was no point celebrating Christmas, and she made sure everyone was as miserable as she was.

When Kara was married to Danny, he always overspent at Christmas, leaving her to struggle with all the bills in January. It had been difficult to be excited about the holidays under those circumstances.

This year, though, nothing seemed to suppress her pleasure in the season. Cole's aunt Shirley brought her a dozen stained glass cookie ornaments, the Hobsons sent her a Christmas floral arrangement contained in a colorful sleigh with a card that thanked Kara for allowing Blaine to take so much of her time, and her students pitched in and bought her a black cardigan embroidered with snowflakes and stars. Life had never been so good.

With the money she'd saved from her job as a hang-gliding instructor, she bought Taylor a simple computer setup, and a computer game that involved building a trucking empire. For Mel she purchased a long mesh stocking filled with dog treats, and she made Cole a coupon book of catered meals. She'd racked her brain to think of the right thing for him, then remembered that he'd teased her about his being willing to do almost anything for her food.

She sighed as she used her best calligraphy to create a certificate promising a pot of country ribs, sauerkraut and potatoes. What she'd give if he *hadn't* been kidding about doing *anything*.

COLE WALKED THE FLOOR with his screaming nephew, singing an off-key rendition of "Here Comes Santa Claus." Little Brad was not at all impressed by Cole's attempts to quiet him.

"Look, I'm doing my best here, pal. Making babies is a clear concept in my mind, but dealing with them once they've arrived is something else again. But you're here now and there's no going back, okay? And the best thing you can do for yourself is resist any temptation to act like your father. It just won't fly with me. He carried on a lot, too, when we were kids, but I just ignored him."

Cole shifted the still-screaming baby to his other shoulder and kept pacing. "But you're a cute little kid. I could make an exception and get you that bottle of juice your mom left for you, but I want a guarantee that it's going to make you stop screaming. The milk didn't do it, and the rocking didn't do it. I'm out of ideas. Help me out, kid."

Cole went to the kitchen for the juice, ran the bottle under the hot water the way Emily had showed him, then put it to Brad's lips. The baby took two pulls on the bottle, then screwed up his little face again and screamed bloody murder.

Emily had left a number where she and Brad could be reached, but Cole was determined not to ruin their night out together. Mel had gone to hide in the bedroom, and Cole suspected everyone within a mile radius was wearing ear protectors.

He went to the desk to dial his aunt Shirley. He had the phone to his ear and was stabbing out the number when he stopped. He could hear again! Little Brad had stopped screaming.

Cole put down the phone and held the baby up in front of him, expecting to see him turning blue.

Actually, his wide dark eyes were focused somewhere over Cole's shoulder, his little mouth was pursed, and two chubby arms flapped in excitement.

Cole turned to see what had captured the baby's attention.

The tree!

The baby was as fascinated by Cole's Christmas tree as everyone else. Cole wouldn't have been surprised if the baby said, *"You never put up a tree!"*

But the only sound coming out of his pursed lips was a high-pitched cooing.

Cole carried the baby closer to the tree. He pointed out the cookie decorations his aunt had made, showed Brad the ornament that looked like Mel, the garland Kara had admired, the angel for the top. The angel still stood on the desk because Cole wouldn't put it up until Taylor could do it, and Cole's schedule had been out of sync with Kara's all week.

The baby's eyelids closed sleepily once, and he began to whine again. Cole put the juice bottle to his lips and he sucked. With the rocker just a few steps away, Cole wrapped the blanket a little more snugly around the baby and began to hum another carol. Sinking farther into the rocker, he prayed that this time his efforts would combine to send his charming but noisy nephew to Dreamland.

Mel wandered out of the bedroom, sniffed the baby in Cole's arms, then curled up on the floor beside the chair.

In that moment of quiet, little Brad snuggling into

him and making greedy, contented noises, Cole experienced an extraordinary sense of accomplishment unmatched by any of his achievements as a police officer. He'd comforted a crying baby. Wow.

Then his thoughts turned to his own baby. For a moment he was overwhelmed by a sense of loss. It continued to amaze him that he could feel so much for a life that was never realized, but he did. And then all the other questions piled on top. Angela must have known, or at least suspected, she was pregnant. How could she not have told him? How could she simply have made plans to leave when a life they'd created together was unfurling inside her?

His practical brain gave him the same reply it had been giving him for three years. Angela and the baby were both gone, making answers to those questions unnecessary.

But if he wanted a relationship with Kara, he had to come to some conclusion that would convince him that things would be different with her, that he would inspire more love and loyalty with her than he had with Angela.

Brad watched him with sleepy eyes as he continued to guzzle the juice, his tiny fingers opening and closing in what looked like some mysterious sign language. Cole touched the baby's fingers with one of his and found himself caught in a sudden death grip. Heavy eyelids closed and the juice bottle fell out of Brad's mouth to the floor, bonking Mel on the nose. Having been through long chases, challenging searches and even gun battles, Mel simply moved his head over an inch, unaffected by the assault.

"Great, Brad," Cole said softly. "Now what am I supposed to do? Boil it? Sanitize it in a little brandy? Actually, that's not a bad idea, is it. Maybe we'll both have to try that."

Cole's brother and his wife were shocked when Cole greeted them at the door shortly after midnight, the baby happily asleep in his arm. Mel barked a welcome. Emily, tall and elegant with rich brown hair and amber eyes, leaned down to pet the dog, then stared at her baby, looking pleased.

"Did he give you any trouble?" she asked Cole in amazement. "He doesn't sleep like this for *me*." She took the baby from him, careful not to wake him.

Brad leaned closer to his son. "You sedated him, didn't you? The two of you have been drinking together. Tell me the truth."

Cole slung the colorful diaper bag over his brother's shoulder. "Clever boy obviously takes after his uncle. Likes my Christmas tree."

"How do you know?" Brad asked.

"He told me," Cole replied.

Emily reached up to kiss Cole's cheek. "Thank you, Cole. We had a beautiful evening." She and Brad shared a look filled with love and adoration.

"Oh, go home!" Cole teased. "I'm glad you had a good time but I'm not doing this every night."

"Thanks so much," Brad said with rare gravity. "You like him, don't you?"

"Yeah," Cole said, "he's cool."

"Hmm. Takes after his uncle. Good night."

"Wait." Cole followed them onto the walk, Mel right beside him. "I was thinking we'd have Christmas here. What do you think?"

Both stared at him, then looked at each other. "You mean dinner?" Emily finally asked.

"Yeah," he said. "You and Aunt Shirley can cook, and I'd like to invite Kara and her son. I've got lots of room and—" he waved a hand behind him in the direction of the tree, which glowed in the shadows of the house "—the perfect setting."

"Well…yeah," Brad agreed, and Emily nodded. "But you're sure you want to go to all that trouble?"

"No trouble. Why don't you and Aunt Shirley talk it over, Emily? And if Kara can come, I know she'll want to help out. She's a great cook."

Brad looked at his brother closely. "Are you in love, or have you gone crazy?"

Cole had to think about that. "A little bit of both, I think. Good night." He reached out to touch his nephew's head. "Great job on this baby, guys."

Brad still wore that probing look. "You're okay, right?"

"Of course."

"Good." Brad smiled. "Thanks again. Looks like a great Christmas for the Winslows."

Mel ran into the house and Cole followed, closing the door behind him. Mel waited for Cole near the tree, his rubber ball in his mouth, tail wagging furiously. The dog always got a second wind when Cole was ready to go to bed.

Cole sat on the floor and tossed the ball for Mel a few times. Mel kept retrieving it and dropping it in Cole's lap, dancing excitedly as he waited for Cole to throw it again.

Eventually tiring of the game, Mel ignored the ball and came to lie beside Cole, dropping his head on Cole's thigh and heaving a great sigh. Cole stroked the dog's wiry coat and stared at their spectacular tree.

Kara had been right. There was something magical about having a tree. It affected his mood, his outlook, and even shook off a few of his fears, so that areas of his life that he'd previously thought blocked now seemed to open up.

The thought of spending time with Kara tomorrow filled him with a rush of exhilaration.

Finally he unplugged the tree and headed for bed. Mel followed, curling up in his crate in the bedroom.

As he drifted off to sleep, Cole remembered Brad's words: *"Looks like a great Christmas for the Winslows."*

COLE LOOKED GORGEOUS. Dressed in jeans and a dark blue sweater over a chambray shirt, he stood staring up at her roof, where the reindeer were still unlit.

"Forgot the lights," she said, and ran inside to flip

the switch. Then she locked the door behind her. "Thanks again for doing that." She handed him a coffee cake covered in plastic wrap with a holiday pattern.

"For me?" he asked, looking pleased.

"No," she replied heartlessly. "For Brad. It was nice of him to give up his free time to help you."

"Well…I gave up free time, too."

"Now, don't whine. You also gave me a heart attack and took several years off my life. Then you yelled at me."

"You had it coming. Promise me you'll never confront an intruder again."

"I'm mistress of my own home, sole protector of my son," she said, accepting his hand-up into the passenger seat of his truck. "There are a lot of things I have to handle on my own." She could handle her life on her own, but she didn't want to. She wanted him in it.

Frowning, he closed her door, then headed around to his side and climbed in. "That's not one of them. That's what the police are for. Courage Bay Bar and Grill okay for breakfast?" He placed the coffee cake on top of the jump seat in the back.

"My favorite place."

"Good. We can argue more over bacon and eggs."

Instead, as they sat over breakfast, he told her about baby-sitting his nephew. After their food arrived he went on with pride about surviving a lengthy screaming episode, and told her that the Christmas tree had finally distracted the baby and brought about peace and quiet. As he spoke about his nephew, she detected a glimmer of sadness in his eyes, and could only guess that caring for his brother's baby had led to thoughts of his own.

"Congratulations," she said, wanting to lighten the mood. "Even experienced mothers can have real difficulty with prolonged screaming. It's almost impossible to figure out what point a baby's trying to make when your brain is muddled from the noise and the guilt you feel because you can't stop the crying."

"I do feel very superior," he admitted with a grin.

"And well you should. What's your first stop today?"

"My shopping's finished. I'm just here to fetch and carry for you."

She frowned at him, guilt nudging her. "That's not right. I'm sure there are a lot of things you need to do for yourself on your time off."

Now he frowned at her, apparently as surprised by her curious reluctance to connect with him as she was by his cheerful, open behavior.

"No, there aren't," he said. "Being with you is a priority." Then he added unexpectedly, "I'd like you and Taylor to join us for Christmas."

"Us?" she repeated.

"My aunt and my brother and his family."

This was a bit of a shock. "Let me guess," she said, trying to sort out her conflicting feelings. "I have to bring my coffee cake."

He didn't react, but she saw the wariness in his eyes. "Only if you want to. What's going on, Kara?"

She pretended innocence. "What do you mean?"

"Something's bothering you."

"No," she lied, toasting him with her coffee cup. "But if you're here just to help me out, then I'm buying lunch."

"Tully's has chili fries and monster chocolate sundaes," he told her, apparently willing to accept her offer.

Kara was grateful he didn't press her about her reaction to his invitation. She knew she should be thrilled at the prospect of spending Christmas with Cole and his family, but for some reason she felt vulnerable. Not to mention guilty that she couldn't just come out and tell him about Loren.

It wouldn't be fair not to go with Loren. She just hoped that Cole never found out and that Loren realized his was just an evening out between friends. What on earth had she been thinking when she'd said yes?

The sooner this evening came and went, the better. She was beginning to think her marriage to Danny had left her more messed up when it came to men than she'd thought.

"You're sure there's nothing wrong?" he asked again. "You look as though you've been given a choice between hanging and a firing squad."

That was exactly how she felt.

Determined to enjoy this morning, and her time with Cole, she fibbed—again. "Actually, it's a choice between Christmas socks and movie gift certificates for the kids in my chorus. What do you think?"

He studied her for a moment as though uncertain

whether to believe her. But he didn't question her. "Hard to go wrong with gift certificates," he counseled. "Then again, they could hang up the socks on Christmas Eve and possibly get *more* stuff."

She laughed at that mercenary thought and decided her students would likely endorse it.

COLE FOLLOWED KARA patiently from store to store, never complaining when she lingered, offering an opinion when she asked for it. At the toy store, he advised her against the galaxy freighter Air Athlete in favor of the Gamma Quadrant patrol ship.

"Taylor prefers the patrol ship," he told her. "He helped me buy one for Blaine."

"Really." She put the freighter back and picked up the one Cole offered her. "I wonder why."

"You wouldn't want to know." He followed her to the counter with two large shopping bags filled with purchases. "It's very sexist."

She looked alarmed. "No! I've raised him not to be sexist."

He shrugged. "He's a guy. He can't help the inclination toward action, which the patrol ship would have over the freighter."

She was puzzled. "That's not sexist."

"No. But the notion that a quarterback attracts more babes than a hitter is."

She gasped indignantly. "*Babes?* He used the word *babes*?"

"I suggested he use the word *women* from now on."

"Thank you."

"You're welcome."

She paid for the purchase and he followed her out into the mall. "Do quarterbacks really get more women than hitters?" she asked.

The question seemed to amuse him. "Never having been either, I can only go on hearsay. Football's about muscle, and baseball's about brains. As a woman, which would you pick?"

He was looking into her eyes, and his own were filled with laughter and probing interest.

"I've…never really been impressed by athletes. I mean, by their prowess, certainly, but not in terms of sex appeal." As she spoke, she was thinking that policemen were sexy. One in particular.

She knew when his grin widened and he lowered his head to kiss her that he'd read her mind.

"You just keep thinking that," he said.

Sexual tension and guilt were not compatible cohabitants of a woman's being, she decided as they stopped in a shop filled with holiday clothing accessories. Her stomach was beginning to churn. She bought socks decorated with snowmen for the girls and reindeer for the boys.

Her stomach flipped right over when she and Cole walked back out into the mall and almost collided with Loren. He looked pleased to see her, until he noticed Cole.

"Winslow," he said with a barely polite inclination of his head.

"Ford," Cole replied, his courtesy stretched as tightly as Loren's.

Kara couldn't believe this was happening. She'd never been a woman to play games, to pit one man against another. And yet she had a horrible feeling this was going to look like she was doing precisely that.

"What's going on?" Loren asked, his smile taut.

Cole opened his mouth to reply, but afraid of what he might say, she put in quickly, "He's helping me pick out gifts for Taylor. He and Taylor shopped together last week for Cole's neighbor's son, and I thought I'd put what he learned to good use." Both men looked a little surprised at her rambling reply.

"You shopping, too?" she asked Loren cheerfully, as though unaware of the mounting tension.

His armload of bags made the question silly.

"I thought you might be getting ready for tonight," Loren said.

Oh, no. "It doesn't take me long," she replied brightly. "I've got my routine."

A heavy silence fell over their little group, and Kara couldn't bear the tension. She was just about to say that she had to go meet Taylor when Cole asked with quiet menace, "What are you getting ready for, Kara?"

Before she could reply, Loren said, "I'm taking Kara to the city's Christmas Ball."

Cole turned slowly to her. "Really."

She sighed, sexual tension and guilt now rubbing against each other like sticks, creating a fire in her stomach. "Yes, really. Well..." She was about to explain that she and Loren were going to the dance as friends, but she had an uneasy feeling that Loren might contradict her.

"Loren, I'll see you tonight," she said firmly, smiling at him. After all, this whole thing was her fault, not his.

He looked dubiously from her to Cole. "You want me to take you home now?"

"No. I'll see you tonight."

"Okay. I'll pick you up at seven-thirty."

"I'll be ready."

"So will I."

Kara didn't think she was imagining the suggestive tone underlying those three simple words.

With a swift, superior glance aimed at Cole, Loren walked away.

Cole didn't move, except to put her shopping bags down. His face was filled with anger and confusion. She was sure his feelings were hurt.

"I can explain," she said.

"Can you?"

Kara wasn't so sure anymore. It was becoming harder to remember what *had* pushed her to accept Loren's invitation.

"Loren's been asking me to go to the ball with him for weeks," she said, meeting Cole's eyes with what she hoped was intrepid honesty.

"So...whether or not you agree to go somewhere depends on the number of times you're asked?"

The question was annoying, but Kara figured she owed Cole a response.

"No," she replied calmly, "but I don't know why it seems to bother you that I said yes. You've made it clear you don't want to get serious with—"

"I didn't say that," he interrupted. "I said I couldn't do it right now...."

"Well, right now is all we've got. I need to get on with my—"

"What, are you on some sort of schedule?" he demanded angrily. "I think you're pushing so hard because you want someone you can pin down. You could never trust Danny, so when I come along and seem trustworthy, you want to staple me in his place."

Kara was so stunned she couldn't speak for a moment. "I don't need you to psychoanalyze me, Cole."

"Well, it's time somebody did," he pointed out harshly.

Tears of frustration stung Kara's eyes, but the last thing she wanted was to let them fall.

"You need to start by being honest with yourself, and with Taylor. Your son deserves to know that his father chose crime over his family, so he doesn't hate the first man who comes into your life and tries to stand in his place. Taylor needs a man in his life—but Loren Ford? Come on..."

Kara was growing angry now. "You have no right to criticize Loren. He's a good administrator—"

"If you say he does his job well, I believe you. But Loren's got an overinflated ego. Do you and Taylor need another Danny in your lives?"

Kara whirled around and stormed away, too angry and too close to tears to respond. Of course she didn't want Loren in her life, and right now she wasn't so sure about Cole, either.

Strong fingers caught her arm on the sidewalk just outside the mall. In a fury, she yanked away, and Cole held his hand up to assure her he wouldn't try to detain her. In his other hand were the shopping bags she'd left behind.

"You forgot these," he said.

She tried to take them from him, but he held them away.

"Where do you think you're going?" he demanded, sounding as if he was barely holding his temper in check. "We came in my truck, remember? And you're supposed to work the fair in—" he checked his watch "—an hour."

Remembering that this was all her fault, Kara tried to stop their spiraling anger and explain. "Cole, I'm sorry. I guess I just don't know how to deal with you."

"Fine," he said. "I'll save you the trouble."

He began to walk away, but she caught his arm and pulled him toward a quiet corner.

"This is just great!" she said. "You can just go off and live your big heroic life all alone, because you're afraid if you let a woman come close again, she'll just hurt you the way your wife did."

"At least I don't lie to my son, and I've never led anyone on."

"I didn't lead you on!" she whispered harshly. "Far from it! You made me believe there was no hope."

"'Don't think you're getting away from me,'" he said, quoting himself. "Did that sound like there was no hope? And what about the invitation to share Christmas with my family?"

"You didn't extend that invitation until today," she said. "I'd already accepted Loren's invitation."

"After I told you that you weren't getting away from me."

"Those are just teasing expressions, Cole. I'm ready to start my life over, but you're still trying to fix your old one." She drew a breath and tried to think logically. "Cole, I understand about the baby. I lost a baby after Taylor was born. I know it isn't just a cluster of cells. It's part of your soul."

He seemed momentarily off balance, then stiffened again. "So, even though you understand that, your choice was to take up with someone who—"

"I'm not *taking up*." She repeated his words with scornful emphasis. "We're going to a dance. And I said yes to the invitation *before* you told me about the baby."

He was unimpressed with her explanation. "I apologize if my timing was off," he observed stiffly. "I can see that your timetable is everything to you. You might want to think about working on loosening up a bit if you really do plan to have a relationship with anyone."

This was hopeless, Kara realized. "Maybe that's been our whole problem. You're not ready to love me, and I'm not willing to wait. I've wasted most of my life on the wrong man, and I don't want to waste any more time."

"Thank you." He inclined his head. "It's ego-building to be thought of as a waste of time."

Kara didn't entirely understand what had happened. She'd begun the day feeling guilty about going to the dance with Loren, but now she wished she'd taken out a contract on Cole instead. She'd never known anyone who could fill her with joy one moment and despair the next.

"I guess this is it," she said, her voice choked.

Cole looked at his truck, then back at her. Expecting him to storm away, she was surprised when he came to her and caught her chin between his thumb and forefinger.

"If you think you might get serious about Loren, let me give you something for comparison."

He combed his fingers into her hair, cupped her head in his hand and lowered his mouth to kiss her.

Kara saw the kiss coming and tried to steel herself against her usual reaction to his touch. She was successful for about two heartbeats, then the rightness of his mouth on hers and the feel of her body pressed into his made her forget why she should fight it.

At first his mouth and his embrace were angry, then his manner softened, the kiss deepened, and she was lost in the tender power of it.

One hand stroked down her back, moving to shape a hip, then press her to him. She immediately felt his reaction.

He dropped his hands from her, and when she looked up at him, she saw that his anger was back.

"You're not going to get that from Loren," he warned. "He's only passionate about himself. Good-bye, Kara." Turning from her, he made his way toward his truck.

Things would have been so much simpler, Kara concluded in despair, if she'd just fallen to the bottom of the Embrace.

Okay. With a toss of her hair, she shook off the memory of Cole's kiss. The man had issues to deal with, and until he did, she couldn't risk getting involved with him.

Loren might not have any of Cole's appeal as a man, but Kara was determined to enjoy this date for the simple social outing it was. She picked up her bags, groaned at their weight and headed back into the mall, ignoring the tingle that lingered in her mouth and her hair from Cole's touch.

CHAPTER ELEVEN

NOW THAT HIS PRIDE was decimated by Kara's date with Loren Ford, Cole had no problem sitting behind the Grannies' table. It was covered with knitted, crocheted and embroidered crafts, doll clothes, napkins, table covers, and dishcloths with flowers on them. There was also a myriad of baked goods.

His aunt and her friends had gone off to tour the bazaar together and had promised to return with a corn dog or something to sustain him. Meanwhile, he'd spent a small fortune on their candies and cookies in an attempt to ward off his misery.

His friend Gehlen appeared, looked over the wares, and asked with apparent sincerity, "You made all this yourself? On stakeouts, no doubt."

"Funny," Cole replied. "You know your mom baked all the cookies."

"Yeah. She wouldn't give me any. Said I had to come and buy them. How long do you have to sit here? This isn't exactly a high-adventure afternoon."

"I promised to help out. How come you don't have to?"

Gehlen picked up a plate of brownies and studied it carefully. "Because I'm here with Wanda, and Mom's thrilled about it. Wanda's working an hour at the library's booth."

It took a moment for that to sink in. Gehlen and the police department's favorite dispatcher? "You're here with Wanda?" Cole asked in disbelief. "You mean…together?"

Gehlen didn't seem to understand his surprise. "Yeah. We've been out a couple of times. I'm taking her to the Christmas Ball tonight."

Cole couldn't stop staring. "I can't believe it. You actually…noticed her?"

"I *noticed* her a year ago," Gehlen informed him. "But…you know…" Now he was avoiding Cole's eyes. "She represents everything I didn't think I wanted. Two kids. A mortgage. Nine-to-five Monday through Friday, soccer games and ballet lessons on weekends."

"What changed your mind?"

Gehlen shrugged and handed him three dollars for the brownies. "A lot of things. But mostly I remember the day we rescued your pretty music teacher and she gave you that kiss."

"That was rescue exuberance," Cole said.

Shaking his head, Gehlen looked straight at Cole. "Partly, but I think it was more than that. I remember that when she looked in your eyes, it was as though she'd found just what she'd been searching for. As if you represented all kinds of possibilities. I wanted somebody to look at me like that.... You still seeing her?"

Cole put out another plate of brownies to replace the one his friend had bought. "She's going to the ball tonight with Loren Ford," he said.

Gehlen's mouth fell open. "You must have really offended her to make her do that."

Cole stood, desperately needing to stretch. "I don't know. I'm not moving fast enough for her, I think."

"But it's only been...what? Two weeks?"

"Yeah. But there's been something right about it from the beginning. Something that compressed time and connected us from the minute you dropped her into my arms from that tree."

"Then what's your problem?"

"I felt like that once before, and it still went bad."

"But it's like that with most things in life—and especially in our line of work. There's always a risk of something going wrong. It doesn't matter how many hooks and locks you have in place, something can malfunction, a rock can move...you can fall."

"But, we're trained to move carefully to protect ourselves and anyone else on our line from that happening."

"Yes. But if you waited until the outcome was one hundred percent secure, you'd never make the climb."

"Cole!" A boy's voice filled the sudden silence, and Cole looked up to see Taylor, Blaine and Finlay Kirk, Taylor's neighbor, approaching the booth.

"Fudge!" Blaine shouted, picking up a plateful of pale, creamy-looking squares filled with nuts. "Is it peanut butter?"

"It's penuche," Finlay replied. "My grandmother made it. It's yum."

Gehlen offered Cole a parting handshake. "You're the only non-climber I'd ever go climbing with," he said, "because you're smart and you never think just of yourself. You always look at the whole picture. She needs to know that."

"Who?" Taylor asked while Blaine and Finlay pooled their money to buy the plate of fudge.

Cole introduced Taylor to Gehlen. "This is Kara's son, Taylor. And his friends Blaine and Finlay."

"Ah." Gehlen shook hands all around. Finlay, apparently one of the boys despite a very feminine red-and-white Christmas sweater, shook his hand as well.

"We're talking about your mom," Cole said as he waved Gehlen off. "She has to know how good Aunt Shirley's fudge is."

"When are we coming over again?" Taylor asked, sampling a piece of fudge from the plate his friends had already unwrapped.

"Uh…I'm not sure," Cole replied carefully. "You'll have to ask your mom. Sounds like she's pretty busy."

"Did you get a topper for the tree?"

"Yes, I did."

"I'm supposed to put it on, right?"

He'd promised. However things worked out between Kara and him, he had to make that happen.

"Sure. You can ask your mom about it, and if she's too busy to come over, I'll come pick you up."

Taylor studied him suspiciously. "Are you mad at Mom 'cause she's going to a party with Mr. Ford? You guys are supposed to be friends."

"Of course we're friends, just like you and I are friends," Cole assured him. "And Mel's your friend. You don't ever have to worry about that."

The last thing Cole wanted to do was upset Taylor. The poor kid had had enough lies told to him about his father. Somehow Cole had to make sure that whatever went on between him and Kara, Taylor wouldn't be hurt.

SHIRLEY AND HER FRIENDS returned, fussing over Taylor and his companions and forcing more fudge on them, free of charge.

Cole was about to leave when Brad appeared without Emily or the baby.

"Emily and some of her new-mother friends went shopping," he explained. "Then they're going out to dinner, watching chick flicks at somebody's house, and comparing babies. I think the plot is to leave their husbands free to shop for them. You and Kara going to the ball?"

"She's going with Mr. Ford," Taylor piped up.

Brad looked questioningly at Cole. "Mr. Ford?"

Then he seemed to realize who he meant. "Oh, not Loren Ford?" he groaned.

"Don't you like him?" Taylor asked.

Cole frowned at his brother.

"Oh, sure," Brad said, giving an apologetic shrug. Then he turned to Cole. "What happened?"

"She got in a blue snit."

"Pardon me?"

"It's a long story. If you're a bachelor tonight, you want to have dinner? There's a movie at the Cineplex that has cops and doctors in it. There should be a lot to criticize."

"Sure. When?"

"Six-thirty? I'll pick you up."

"Okay."

Cole headed for the games booths at the other end of the field, only to discover that he was being followed by Taylor and his friends.

"Don't you guys have things to do?" he asked.

Taylor shook his head. "Not till tonight. Blaine is having a sleepover for his birthday. Finlay can't come 'cause she's a girl. So me and Blaine are trying to win her a doll at the shooting booth, but you gotta hit six bull's-eyes and we can't do it. Can you try?"

Cole was grumpy and morose, and the last thing he wanted to do was shoot a gun—even an air gun. But the boys were being thoughtful, so how could he refuse.

"Okay. I'll give it a try. Where's the booth?"

He had the doll in six shots. Finlay jumped up and down screaming her delight, and the boys high-fived each other as though they'd won it. The man tending the booth handed over a large doll with lots of long dark hair and petticoat-puffed calico. Finlay beamed—so much for her being one of the boys—and wrapped an arm around Cole.

"Thank you, Cole!" she said, hugging the doll to her. "I can't believe you did it. I got the doll!"

At least one person had gotten what they wanted, Cole thought.

"I have to go show my mom!" she said. "She's working at the Methodist Church booth."

"You guys better go with her," Cole said as she raced off. "She shouldn't be running around alone."

"Thanks, Cole." Taylor smiled with sincere gratitude. "She's pretty cool for a girl."

"I noticed that." Cole watched until the boys caught up with her, then decided he'd had enough Christmas cheer and headed for his truck, and home.

KARA WRAPPED PRESENTS until she was sure she'd used every scrap of paper and every inch of ribbon in the county. Several of her students worked beside her, wrapping in spurts between hanging out with friends, running to other booths for food, taking cell phone calls from friends, then running for more food.

She looked up at one point when she heard a familiar voice and saw her son and his two best friends dancing along beside Cole, obviously headed for the game booths. For several hours, Cole's behavior had managed to completely submerge her earlier regrets at having hurt him, but now her guilt returned with a vengeance.

She watched him smile at something Taylor said, saw her son laugh in response, and found herself wishing she could begin the day over again. There was a giant black hole in the middle of her being, where only two days ago there'd been happiness and hope for her future. And Taylor's.

Cole and the children disappeared in the crowd, and she returned to her wrapping. She was putting a very large bow on a giant, misshapen package that contained a stuffed gorilla when she heard Taylor's voice again. She looked up to see Finlay hugging a large doll and jumping up and down in excitement. Finlay wrapped her arms around Cole and he hugged her lightly in return.

Even in the middle of her divorce proceedings, Kara hadn't felt this depressed. She told herself there was no point feeling bad about the way she and Cole had parted. It didn't change the fact that their goals would never have come together, with or without the issue of Loren.

She watched Finlay run off and saw Cole motion the boys to follow her, a warm expression on his face.

But once the children were out of sight, Cole looked around grimly. Instead of coming back to the bazaar, he dug keys out of his pocket and headed for the parking lot.

The need to intercept him was so powerful, she would have done it—if the owner of the misshapen package hadn't appeared with a crisp five-dollar bill, forcing her to make change.

WHEN KARA WAS WRONG, she was spectacularly wrong, and thinking she might actually enjoy a social evening with Loren was sure to rate right up there with her worst misjudgments.

The setting for the Christmas Ball was perfect. The lobby of City Hall was festooned with fresh evergreen garlands decorated with gold ball ornaments and twinkle lights. Her chorus sang like angels, and the holiday music played by a local band was a fun mix of traditional and more modern tunes.

Kara saw many couples she knew from school, and enjoyed conversations with them while Loren made a few obligatory rounds on the dance floor with members of his staff and the local school board. The champagne and hors d'oeuvres were elegant and delicious.

The only thing wrong with the evening was her assumption that it would be fun to go out with Loren. Even with her track record, she couldn't believe how mistaken she'd been.

During the drive to the hall and the first hour of dancing, he'd talked nonstop about his career plans.

That would have been all right, except that she soon noticed his goals had nothing to do with the students' welfare and everything to do with the advancement of a future political career.

"I can't accomplish what I want in a little place like Courage Bay," he'd said when explaining that his first step was to obtain a superintendent's position. "I have to go to a bigger city where there are more students, a larger budget."

At first Kara had been surprised to hear that. She'd always thought Loren cared about the students at C.B. Junior High. But as he kept talking, she realized that he was more interested in the students performing well because that would be a positive reflection on his administrative skills.

By nine o'clock she was ready to go home. But as she reminded herself, she'd chosen to do this and she had to see it through graciously. Maybe if she took firm hold of the conversation, Loren would have to listen to her for a change.

"I'm so happy that Taylor is finally making friends," she said as Loren led her onto the dance floor for a slow number. "I was so worried about him last year, but now…"

Loren put a silencing finger to her lips. "No talk about children tonight, all right?" he said with smiling good-humor. "I deal with them all day long, and now that I finally have you all to myself, I don't want to talk about kids or work."

She couldn't believe she'd heard him correctly. "Loren, my work and my son are my life."

He nodded. "I know that, and I intend to do something about it if you'll let me. I've seen too many mothers—single and married—become overly involved with their children's lives. Our parents didn't spend half as much time fussing about us, and I think we turned out just fine." He gave her a smug look.

"What?" she demanded.

When she stopped dancing, he tried to drag her along while glancing around to make sure no one had noticed them. "Kara, you're making a scene," he cautioned under his breath.

"'Fussing'!" she exclaimed. "Is that what you call parental involvement? What about all the studies that show a child's performance in school can be directly linked to—"

"I know, I know." He caught both her arms and forced her into a dance position again, smiling at the other couples twirling by who were starting to stare. "I was talking about overinvolvement. Come on, Kara. Why are you acting like this? It's not doing either of us much good to be seen calling attention to ourselves at a public gathering."

What he really meant was that the head of the school board and his wife were watching.

She smiled politely at him for their benefit. "Loren, I have a headache. I'd like to go home now."

"Kara..." he said in exasperation.

She took a step backward and walked off the dance floor. He followed.

"Fine. I'll take you home." He found her coat and held it open for her. "But we'll stop on the way for a late dinner, so you can explain to me what's happened here. I mean, it was a beautiful evening and suddenly...poof! You explode."

Poof? she thought. It had been more like *blam!*

Of course, Loren probably had had a beautiful evening listening to himself, Kara realized.

When he pulled into an all-night coffee spot on the highway, famous for its all-you-can-eat ribs on Saturday night, she began to wonder if he was completely clueless. How could anyone have a heart-to-heart discussion in a place packed with every barbecue-lover in the county? But she said nothing.

As they walked across the parking lot and into the unpretentious little restaurant, she was ready to believe she'd been born with a gene that prevented her from recognizing men for what they were. She'd thought Danny was an exciting adventurer, but he'd turned out to be a con artist. Loren had seemed so good with kids, but after tonight, Kara wasn't sure if he even liked them, let alone cared about their futures. And Cole, the hero who'd caught her in midair, was secretly afraid of her.

Taylor was the only guy in her life she could count on, and even he'd grow up and leave her one day.

Loren opened the door for her and she walked inside, wondering how she would explain to Loren that accepting his invitation had been a mistake. After all, she still had to work with him.

The restaurant was a square room with booths along the wall and chairs in the middle. At this hour, all the young men with big appetites who frequented the place seemed to be gone, and the restaurant was populated with seniors. The pleasant aroma of a bourbon-based barbecue sauce filled the room. But as Kara reached an empty booth and prepared to slip in, she suddenly felt a palpable tension. Looking around, she realized no one was eating.

Behind the counter, three waitresses stood in a tight little knot. It was impossible to see what was happening behind them in the kitchen, but she could hear shouting.

Then she became aware of the noise. The jukebox was at deafening volume, and a bald man in camouflage was dancing to it with an older woman who appeared terrified.

Another man with long curly hair was sitting at the end of the bar, staring at her.

Kara felt a weird sense of disassociation from reality, as though she were watching herself in a film.

The bald man spun the woman around and stopped abruptly when he saw Kara standing near the booth. Pushing the woman into the nearest chair, he strode across the coffee shop toward Kara.

Her heart rose into her throat. She wondered if these

men were robbing the restaurant. Then she realized that if they were, there wouldn't be time for dancing.

They weren't robbing the place, she decided, just terrorizing the patrons. Neither of the men seemed to have a weapon, and a quick survey of the customers told her they were mostly older couples and teenagers. Not a good match for scary-looking men out to intimidate.

As the bald man drew closer, she turned to Loren and asked under her breath, "Do you have a cell phone?"

But rescue was clearly not going to come from him. He was white as chalk and apparently paralyzed.

When the man reached Kara, he pointed his index finger at Loren. "Sit down!" he ordered.

Loren did just that.

"There, now." The bald man smiled at Kara and closed a hand on her arm. "You're going to dance with me."

She was frightened, but instinct told her that if he knew that, she'd be at more of a disadvantage than she already was.

"Thank you," she said, removing her arm from his grasp, "but I've just come from a dance, and my feet hurt."

Surprisingly he let her go, but when his friend at the end of the bar started to laugh, he grabbed Kara roughly around the waist and held her to him. He smelled of cologne and mouthwash, and though she knew she should feel terrified, she couldn't help observing that good grooming did not seem to be synonymous with good citizenship.

"I said you're going to dance with me!" the bald man shouted in her face.

Fury ignited his eyes, and Kara concluded that he must be high on something or not entirely sane. So, should she cooperate and take her chances that someone had already dialed 911, or refuse to behave like a victim because she was quite possibly on her own here and her wits were the only tool she had?

"I said my feet hurt!" she shouted back at him. "And I'm not moving from this booth until I've had a cup of coffee!"

CHAPTER TWELVE

COLE AND BRAD headed home in Brad's vehicle, a little quiet because the movie had been more accurate than not and there'd been little in it to complain about.

"Maybe she did it to make you jealous?" Brad suggested as he pulled up at a stoplight. Cole had told Brad about Kara's date with Loren when they left the theater.

"No." Cole scanned the streets out of habit, just as he did while on patrol. "Kara would never be that conniving. But there's no hope for either of us. We're obviously both failures when it comes to marriage."

Brad turned to look at him. "Cole, that is so much bull!" he slapped the steering wheel and focused on the road once more. "What's happened to your brain? You're not the first one to make a bad choice when it comes to marriage, but get over it, for God's sake. This time you might just get it right. If you're using the past as a way to avoid living again, then you really are in big trouble. You can't just give up."

The light changed and Brad drove on. "I can't believe I have to explain that to you when you're the one who kept me going through high school and college and medical school. How many times would I have quit if you hadn't reminded me that anything worth having requires hard work? And that goes for personal relationships, too."

Cole turned in mild surprise to study his brother's profile. Brad had always had a serious turn of mind, been a good, conscientious student, a responsible man, but becoming a father seemed to have added another dimension to his character.

"I have no idea what's real or right anymore," Cole said honestly. "But I'm glad to see you've got your head straight about what's important in life."

"You do, too," Brad said with a grin in his direction. "You're just momentarily stymied by feelings that are bigger than you. You don't like that. You can't arrest it, put it in jail, testify against it. It just stays right there beside you, reminding you every day that you can't take charge of everything— Want to stop for ribs?"

Brad pulled into the parking lot of Midnight Coffee, the best place to get something to eat at this hour. And the only place in town with a "rib night" that lasted from five o'clock to midnight. It was a local favorite on Saturday nights.

Cole was about to tell him that he didn't want to stop, but Brad was already parking near the front. Then—unbelievably—Cole spotted Kara through the window of the coffee shop. She was wearing a red dress that clung to her small waist and left her shoulders bare.

Profound jealousy swelled in him when he saw that Loren had a firm grip on her arm and was looking into her eyes. But then his brain recognized something wrong with the picture. The guy was bald and not the blow-dried sophisticate that Loren was. And he was a couple of inches taller as well.

As Cole climbed out of the car, he saw Kara pull away from the man. And suddenly, even from outside the restaurant, he saw fear—in Kara, in Loren, whom he finally spotted slouched in the booth across from her, in the faces of the other customers. No one was eating. Everyone was watching the little drama playing out in Kara's booth.

Cole focused on the bald guy, thinking he looked familiar. Scanning the parking lot, Cole picked out his vehicle, a beat-up black Jeep with a tarantula hanging from the rearview mirror.

Cole directed Brad back to the car as his brother locked it with his remote. "Something's going on inside," he said, hurrying toward the door. "Radio for backup!"

As he opened the restaurant door, he heard Brad call, "I don't *have* a radio."

True. He didn't. Great time, Cole thought, to forget I'm not on duty.

But he was already halfway inside, and Calvin Bishop, petty thief, part-time drug dealer and major crazy, was pulling Kara by the hair and screaming profanities into her face.

"You will dance with me, you…!"

Cole was starting toward him when he was waylaid by a curly-haired kid who leaped off the end of the counter and planted himself in Cole's path.

"Slow down, dude," the kid said. In his hand was a kitchen knife with an impressive serrated blade. "Cal's got something going on, and we don't want to get in his way." He raised the knife toward Cole's throat. "So just sit down, be quiet—"

Cole caught the kid's wrist and bent it backward, sending the knife to the floor, then laid him out with one punch. People were now standing in their booths, and Cole heard a collective gasp.

Calvin Bishop held Kara in front of him, one arm around her waist. His expression sent a chill through Cole. Any sane man faced with confrontation would look alert, even a little afraid. Only a psychopath or someone strung out on drugs had no fear.

Cole caught Kara's eyes for just an instant and saw that she seemed relieved he was there. He had to look away and focus on Bishop or her faith in him wouldn't be justified.

"What's the plan?" he asked Bishop.

"Well, Winslow," Bishop replied. "What's it been? Three months?"

"Not nearly long enough," Cole replied, taking inventory of his surroundings. A table of older ladies behind Bishop. A teenage couple on one side. Not a field of advantage. "It was your last DUI. I pulled you over and you rabbited."

"You chased me for half a mile and took me down in dog crap."

"Seemed appropriate."

Bishop's expression sharpened and turned to anger. He tightened his grip on Kara. When she winced, Cole had to force himself to remain still.

"This lady mean something to you?" Bishop asked.

"No." Cole was careful not to look at her. "Just don't like to see you manhandling anybody." Over Bishop's shoulder, he saw the side door of the restaurant open slowly.

Cole saw Bishop's eyes flick up at the same moment that someone shouted, "Look out!"

His fist already drawn back, Cole turned and punched a fair-haired young man in the stomach. He must have come from the kitchen. A heavy man, he dropped like a stone, a roasting fork clattering to the floor beside Cole.

Cole swung around again to see Bishop retreating. He was holding Kara so tightly that her feet were almost off the floor, and behind him, Brad advanced soundlessly into the room.

Kara was beginning to look panicked. One of her hands reached unconsciously toward Cole.

"She *is* yours!" Bishop accused Cole. "I knew it. I could tell when you walked in. If you don't want me to break her neck—" he put his free hand against Kara's throat "—you'll stay right where you are."

Cole stayed where he was, but Brad continued to advance. He was now within arm's reach of Bishop.

Determination flashed in Kara's eyes. He tried to warn her with a look that help was imminent, but she began to struggle, unaware that her movement pulled Bishop farther from Brad.

But she apparently didn't need Brad. Or him, for that matter, Cole quickly realized. As Bishop attempted to secure his hold on her, Kara brought a high-heeled shoe down hard on his right foot.

With a howl, Bishop doubled over, and she jabbed her elbow into his face. Brad finished the job with the garbage can lid he'd carried in with him. The sound of skull meeting metal reverberated like the sound of a gong.

All Cole had to do was catch Kara as she flew into his arms.

Applause and shouts of approval filled the restaurant. Customers converged on the other two men who were down and held them, along with Bishop, while Cole's backup streamed into the restaurant.

Brad grinned at Cole. "How's Xena?" he asked, touching Kara's shoulder.

To Cole's complete surprise, she was sobbing. Not just crying, but sobbing. For a woman who'd remained calm through a frightening ordeal, Kara seemed to have completely lost it.

He walked her to the door while Brad stayed behind to talk to the police, who were already dealing with a dozen witnesses, all trying to explain what had happened. Loren came over to make sure Kara was unharmed, but when he offered to drive her home, she shook her head. Cole actually felt sorry for him. Loren looked shell-shocked, and Cole spoke to the officer standing just outside the door, asking him to make sure Loren was checked out by the arriving paramedics before he got behind the wheel of his car.

Once he'd directed Kara outside, Cole found a shadowy spot near a tall camellia bush and wrapped both arms around her.

"It's all right," he said quietly, rubbing her back. "It's over. Nobody's hurt. You were a real heroine."

She pushed him away, yet her eyes were sad and tear-filled. He spread both arms out to his sides, confused.

"I wasn't a heroine," she said, still sobbing. "You stormed in there like…like Clint Eastwood and made me believe everything was going to be all right. That gave me the courage to help make it happen."

He was trying hard to see the problem here. "Okay. And now everything is all right. So why…?"

"It's all right in there!" She jabbed an index finger in the direction of the restaurant. "But it's never going to be all right in here!" She punched herself in the heart so hard he half expected her to fall down.

"Why not?" he asked.

At his question, she came unglued.

SHE WAS GOING to have to punch him, Kara thought. Nothing else would relieve the urge she felt to touch him, coupled with the desperate desire to do him bodily harm.

"Why not?" she screamed at him, thinking her anger would be far more effective if she could just stop crying. But she kept remembering her panic, then the wave of relief she'd felt when she saw him marching toward her and Bishop like some fearless superhero.

At that moment she had known what she had to do. It was as though they were plugged into the same circuit, shared the same source of power.

But it was obvious he couldn't see it, and that left her so totally frustrated she could barely stand it.

"I want a life again, and you don't!" she shouted at him.

He was watching her as though he had no idea what she was talking about. She closed her eyes and dragged in a breath, still sane enough to appreciate that she wasn't making much sense.

"I thought you wanted to be with Ford," he said.

"You know as well as I do that I had no intention of getting involved with Loren. I was just...oh, damn it all. But after tonight, I don't know if I can even be civil to the guy. You were right. He's only interested in Loren Ford."

At least she felt calmer now. Kara sighed. "It doesn't matter."

"I'm sorry," he said. Then he shocked her by asking, "You want to come home with me?"

She blinked. "What?"

"Do you want to come home with me?" he repeated. "Taylor's at a sleepover tonight, isn't he?"

Her heart fluttered, even though her brain was telling her to go slowly. "Yes, he is," she replied. "But you can't believe sex is going to fix what's wrong between us."

With a growl of exasperation, Cole caught her arm and walked her over to a strange car. He opened the door and gave her a slight push inside. "Don't move from there!" he ordered, then loped back into the restaurant.

Through the window she could see him talking to one of the uniformed officers. Then he spoke to Brad, who nodded and handed him something.

When Cole came back, he climbed in and shoved the keys into the ignition.

"Is this Brad's car?" she asked. "We're going to leave him stuck there?"

"Yes, it's his car. No, he isn't stuck there. A friend of mine is going to take him home." He pulled out of the parking lot and into the traffic. It was shortly after eleven, but the city was apparently just coming to life for many people.

Kara regretted shouting at Cole. He had come to her rescue, after all. That thought raised a question.

"How did you know where I was?" she asked.

"I didn't," he replied. "Brad and I had been to a movie and were stopping for coffee on the way home. I saw you and Bishop through the window."

"I gather you've dealt with him before."

"Four or five times."

She shuddered as she recalled the terror she'd felt when Bishop had first put his hands on her, then the relief and disbelief when she'd seen Cole's face.

"You were off duty," she said, not sure what that had to do with anything.

He glanced at her, apparently not sure what she meant, either. Then he shook his head as though something was suddenly clear to him.

"Where you're concerned, I'm never off duty."

"You should have waited for help to arrive," she said self-righteously. "That's what you told me."

"Citizens have to wait for help," he said. "Cops jump in and do what has to be done."

"You didn't even have a butter knife," she teased.

He cast her another glance, this one possessive and smoky and full of promise…or warning—she wasn't sure which.

"It was a restaurant. It was full of them."

"Cole…"

He caught her hand and squeezed it. "You know what? Let's just not talk for a while. Every time we try to talk things through, we misunderstand each other. Let's just go sit in front of my tree and see if we can borrow some of its magic."

"Magic?" she asked, hardly believing she'd heard him.

"You told me it would fill my house and make magic," he said. "I doubted you, but it worked."

"How?"

"Shh. Wait till we get there."

The minute they walked into his house, the fragrance of pine enfolded them. Mel came to greet them, and Cole fussed over him for a minute, then went to the dining room to flip the switch for the Christmas tree.

Kara patted Mel and leaned down to kiss his nose. Then she walked around the tree, admiring how beautiful it looked. Gently she put a fingertip to a bubble light.

"I love these," she said, watching the tiny bubbles rise in the clear cylinder. "But aren't they dangerous?"

"Used to be in the old days, but the new ones are safety approved."

She looked up to see what he'd chosen for the top of the tree and noticed with a frown that it was bare.

Cole pointed to the table where a beautiful angel stood, a banner in her hands that read Love. The word was surrounded by musical notes.

"She's beautiful," Kara said. "But why isn't she on the tree?"

"Because I promised Taylor he could put it up, remember? He said it had to be special."

She did. She could almost recall the conversation verbatim. Cole had told her son that if he put the tree-topper up for him, it would be special.

"Yes, I remember. I guess we haven't been back to put it up." There'd been so many misunderstandings between them, but suddenly she couldn't remember what they were. Nor did they matter in the glow of his beautiful tree. She sat down on the floor and saw that all the gifts she'd wrapped for him were crowded atop her tree skirt.

"So, if I sit right here," she asked, spreading the skirt of her dress around her with care, "the tree will work magic on us?"

"That's my belief." He sat down behind her, bending a knee to support her. He wrapped both arms around her and drew her gently back against him so that her cheek rested against his.

Kara leaned into him, delighting in his warmth and the security she felt in his embrace. Love roared like a fire inside her, but she kept the words to herself and waited.

THE REALIZATION that he was holding Kara Abbott in his arms called for a moment's contemplation, Cole decided. He'd brought her here to be quiet, to think, to borrow a little magic so maybe she would understand what reason didn't seem to be able to make clear to her.

All along he'd been afraid that what he'd felt for Kara had been based on a physical attraction to a beautiful woman who was fun to be with. When he'd seen her caught in Bishop's grip tonight, her life threatened, that fear had disintegrated. In its place was a love that felt as solid as life itself. He struggled for the right words to explain that to Kara.

"Can I say something?" she asked in a whisper.

"Yes," he whispered back teasingly. "You can even say it out loud if you want to."

"Well, I wasn't sure," she said. "I mean, I think my talking has been a lot of the problem. I…I don't want to prevent the magic from working."

"I don't think that can happen. What do you want to say?"

She snuggled in a little closer. "I think I've figured out something."

"What's that?"

"You thought that Angela wanted something you didn't have," she said carefully.

That was no longer true, but it had been. "Yes."

"Well, you're wrong." She turned and looked into his eyes. "You have *everything*." She said the words with humbling conviction. "I can't imagine why she couldn't see that! Cole…"

The sound of his name on her lips erased all the dark doubts he'd held on to for three years. "I think," he said, squeezing her closer, "she just didn't want what I had to offer. It's very simple, really. Maybe ego kept me from realizing that. It's hard to feel so strongly about someone and accept that she just doesn't care. Even when she's carrying your baby."

She wrapped her arms around his neck and kissed him with a tenderness he wanted to absorb.

"I think you just offered it to the wrong woman," she said. "It takes a woman who's lived with a rat to really appreciate Santa Claus."

He leaned back to look into her face. "Santa Claus?"

"Oh, Cole—"

There was that reverence in her voice again.

"You restored my faith in men as a species." She grinned. "Loren shook it a little tonight, but then you were there again, catching me in midair." She sobered suddenly and said with conviction, "I will love you forever, whether or not you can love me."

"Kara, I didn't rescue you this time," he pointed out, wondering how she kept missing that detail. "You saved yourself."

"Because you were there!" she said emphatically. "I took one look at your face and knew that whatever it took, you'd make everything turn out right. You inspire confidence in me. I can't help it. So, that's what your magical Christmas tree has drawn out of me. Love for you—and complete faith in you."

That was a lot to live up to, but it was hard to feel inadequate when you were loved that much.

"So," he asked, kissing her quickly, "can you see yourself as Mrs. Claus?"

The light in her eyes was all he needed for Christmas. He wasn't sure what to do about the tears, though. He grabbed the cotton throw from the rocker and eased her down onto it, following her to the floor since she had a death grip on his neck.

"This isn't a sugar-plum dream, is it?" she demanded as he lay beside her.

Her gold necklace picked up the tree lights and her skin appeared to shimmer. He placed his lips at the base of her throat.

"It's Christmas-morning-Santa's-been-here reality," he assured her. "Shall we give ourselves each other as a gift?"

When she placed her hands on his forearms and pushed him slightly away, he experienced a moment's fear.

"You're not forgetting Taylor?" she asked worriedly.

He didn't understand the question. "What do you mean? How could I forget Taylor?"

"He wants his father to come back."

Cole decided this was not the right time to talk about the lie she'd told her son.

"He likes me," he said, "and I like him. We'll work it out."

"He's a great kid," she said, smiling now. "You'll be so good for him."

"I know he is. I'm sold on both of you. And you haven't forgotten Mel?"

ID, license and rabies inoculation tags rattled together in the corner of the room as Mel raised his head.

"Sleep, Mel," Cole said, and the dog settled down again.

Kara laughed quietly. "How could I forget him? He's bigger than Taylor. He's not going to tell anyone what he sees tonight, is he?"

"He's a model of discretion, so we don't have to be."

And they weren't. They undressed each other with gentle efficiency, then made love like two lost souls who had finally found each other.

Cole explored Kara's body as though she were a precious gift, and she approached his with the same care and tenderness.

Although he'd intended to make love to her slowly, Kara seemed determined to move as quickly as she could to show him how deeply and completely she loved him.

When they came together a second time, he made her slow down, urging her to take time, making her plead for the passion he held out of reach for just a while longer.

"You're a monster!" she accused in a whisper as he held her hands in one of his and drove her wild with the other.

He kissed the quivering tip of a breast. "You should know that before you promise 'till death do us part.'"

She ran a knee up the side of his bare thigh. "Just wait till I get you..."

"You already have, and you weren't very merciful, as I recall."

"I was trying to show you," she said on a little moan, "how much I love you."

"That's all I'm trying to do."

"Cole, please. Now!"

He entered her slowly, enjoying her desperation to sheath him completely, then listening for the little moan she made that told him he was worth waiting for.

It was a long time before they lay quietly on the throw, wrapped around each other, limbs and heart-beats entwined.

"Want to move to the bed?" he asked lazily.

She was curled into his side, looking up at the tree, her eyes reflecting the colorful lights. "But the miracle tree is out here."

"True. I'll get a blanket and a couple of pillows."

"No, don't go—"

She threw a leg over him, and he wouldn't have moved for a million dollars.

"I love you," she whispered, then planted a kiss at his collarbone. "I love you so much."

He kissed her hair, thinking he'd remember forever the feel of it caressing his skin as she kissed her way down his body. "I love you, too. What a Christmas."

CHAPTER THIRTEEN

COLE AWOKE to the ringing of the phone. He glanced at his watch by the light of the tree and read that it was just after midnight. Brad, probably, wondering when he could reclaim his car.

He covered a protesting Kara with the throw and went to the phone on the desk. He prayed the department didn't need him to cover a shift.

"Hello?"

"Cole?"

He didn't recognize the anxious voice. "Yes."

"Cole, it's Cindy. Taylor Abbott's here at Blaine's birthday sleepover."

"Yeah."

"Do you know where his mom is?"

Cole felt a flicker of alarm. "She's here with me. Is he okay?"

Kara sat up instantly, worried eyes peering out from disheveled bangs. Then she was on her feet, the throw wrapped around her.

"Well, physically he's fine, but something's upset him. He wants to go home."

"Hold on." Cole handed Kara the phone. "It's Cindy, Blaine's mom. Taylor's not hurt, but he's upset about something."

She took the phone from him, and while she spoke with Cindy, Cole hurried into his bedroom to pull on jeans and a sweatshirt. He brought out a sweatsuit for Kara.

"Here, this should fit you if you cuff the sleeves and roll up the waist," he said as she hung up the phone. "Want me to go next door and get him?"

Kara quickly slipped the clothes on, her expression stricken. "She says Taylor got up to go to the bathroom and found a newspaper her husband brought back from a business trip to San Francisco."

He waited for her to explain further.

She closed her eyes for a moment. "There was an article in it about Danny being denied parole. The real estate scam was big news in San Francisco, so I guess it made the papers."

"You're kidding!" He knew she wasn't, of course. Fate played dirty every chance it got. "Does Taylor even know what parole is?"

She spread her hands helplessly. "He knows it means his father isn't in the military in Europe. I'm going to get him."

"I'll come with you."

KARA FOLLOWED COLE across his driveway to the Hobsons' house. The door opened as they approached, and

Cindy, in a red velour robe, stood in the doorway with a tearful Taylor. Even under the dim porch light, Kara could see the sense of betrayal in her son's eyes, and he was pressing his lips firmly together so he wouldn't cry. Blaine and his friends were lined up in concern behind him, a small army in various superhero pajamas. Behind them was a tall, fair-haired man whom Cindy introduced as her husband, Mark.

"Taylor..." Kara opened her arms to him, but he backed away from her.

He looked up at Cole and said firmly, "I want to go home."

"You got it, buddy. Come on." Cole put a hand to his shoulder and Taylor allowed himself to be led outside. On the doorstep, Kara turned to thank Cindy and apologize for the midnight disturbance.

"That's not a problem," Cindy assured her. "He's welcome back anytime. Right, guys?"

There was a chorus of approval from the superhero army.

Mark came forward, his expression contrite. "I can't believe I was so careless," he said. "I saw the name and meant to ask Cindy out of simple curiosity if... I should never have left the paper—"

Kara forestalled him. "No need to apologize. This isn't your fault. It's mine."

But he looked as though he felt as guilty as she did.

After thanking the Hobsons again, Kara followed

Cole and her son back across the driveway, her guilt large enough to burst out of her body like the alien.

"How come you're at Cole's house?" Taylor asked Kara when she joined him in the living room.

She sat on the edge of the sofa and tried to draw him to her, but he backed away again.

"I said I want to go home." Mel came to nudge Taylor with his nose.

"Before you go, I'll make some cocoa," Cole said. "Come on, Mel." They disappeared into the kitchen.

Kara struggled to remain calm. This was all her fault; now she had to do the best she could to salvage her son's trust.

"Mr. Ford and I didn't really enjoy each other's company, and I met Cole on the way home." It was an abbreviated, sanitized version of what had happened, but still true. "He brought me here to show me his Christmas tree."

Taylor seemed to accept that explanation, then went to his backpack and pulled out a folded page from a newspaper. "Mr. Hobson went to San Francisco for a meeting," he said, handing her the paper, "and he brought this home."

Kara studied the folded paper, seeing vital statistics—births, deaths, accidents.

"It's on the other page." Taylor came to open it for her. He pointed to an article near the middle of the page. The headline read, "Abbott Denied Parole."

"I noticed it because it's our name. Then I read it. Daniel Xavier Abbott. That's Dad."

Kara folded the paper and looked into his face. The anger and sense of betrayal were painful to see. "Yes, it is. I'm sorry I didn't tell you the truth, Taylor. I—"

"What's parole?" he interrupted.

"When someone's in jail," she explained, feeling as though she had to gasp for breath, "they get a chance to get out early if they've obeyed all the rules and learned from their mistakes." She tried to reach for him again and he pulled away.

"You said he was in Germany! You told me he was a hero!"

Kara nodded grimly. "I know. I'm sorry, but I was afraid it would really hurt you to know that he'd cheated people out of their money and gone to jail. You love him so much, I knew it was hard enough for you to have to live without him. I thought if you knew the truth, you'd be hurt even more."

A large tear rolled down Taylor's face and his mouth trembled. He remained stiffly out of her reach. "I told everybody my dad was in the army fighting bad guys! I told them he was really brave. We named one of Blaine's G.I. Joe guys after him."

Kara nodded apologetically. "I made a bad mistake, Taylor. But what your dad did has nothing to do with you. Nobody can hold it against you."

"Oh yeah? Blaine's dad is a lawyer. Kevin's dad is

a reporter, Ernesto's dad owns a gardening business, and Miko's dad helps babies be born."

"You got a bad break with your dad," Kara said. "He has a very good brain. He could have been any one of those things, but he wanted everything to be easy. He didn't want to have to work hard, so he tried to make a lot of money by cheating."

Taylor sank onto the hassock across the room, still glaring at her as large tears fell. "Didn't he know that'd make everybody laugh at us?"

"I don't think he thought about us," she said honestly.

"I know he doesn't like me. I'm too big and I'm no good at sports."

Kara felt a large hand close over her heart. She crossed the distance between them and knelt in front of the hassock. Taylor turned his face away. "Taylor," she said, putting her hands on his arms, relieved when he didn't resist her, "your father loved you very much. He just wasn't…mature enough to think about how what he wanted to do would affect you."

"I loved him," he said sadly. "I thought if I loved him, he'd want to come back."

"I know you love him, sweetheart. And it's okay to still love him if you want to. But you have to understand what he's really like, and not just what you want him to be like."

"You should have told me," he accused, fresh tears falling.

She could no longer hold back her own tears. "I know. And I'm so sorry."

"I want to go home," he said plaintively. "And I don't want to have Christmas."

Gathering up his things, he headed for the door.

She followed him, snatching up her purse, forgetting her clothes. "Taylor, Christmas has nothing to do with what's happened. Christmas is—"

"Christmas is about love and joy and the baby Jesus coming to love all of us." He delivered that insightful assessment of the holiday, then glowered up at her, then at Cole, who stood in the kitchen doorway. "Did you know my dad was in jail?"

"Yes, I did," Cole said.

"How come you didn't tell me? You said we were friends. That I was good to hang out with."

"You are. And when you really like somebody, the last thing you want to do is hurt them. I'm sure your mom would have told you eventually. She was trying to make it easier for you, since you had to move here."

"It's still lying," Taylor said mercilessly. "I'll bet Jesus wouldn't like anybody in our family."

Kara put a hand on Cole's arm as Taylor stormed out the door. She held on to him for a moment, stealing courage from him.

"He just needs the night to think about it," Cole said gently. He reached to the counter for Brad's keys.

The drive home was brief and intensely silent. When they arrived, Taylor climbed out of the car and used his own key to let himself into the house.

"You could have told him you wanted me to tell

him about his father," Kara said, wrapping her arms around Cole.

He hugged her close. "We're going to have to get used to presenting a united front. Want me to try to talk to him?"

She drew away, shaking her head. "No, you're right. He needs time. I love you."

He kissed her. "I love you, too. And that's going to get all of us through. Believe that."

Kara watched him drive away, then went into the house. Taylor's door was closed tightly.

"Do you want some cocoa before bed?" she asked.

"No, thank you," he replied stiffly.

She waited a moment, then called, "I love you."

There was no reply.

COLE NEVER WENT TO BED. He and Mel sat up part of the night drinking coffee and staring at the tree, thinking that its magic had come through for him big-time with Kara. Now he had to make it work with Taylor.

Maybe he'd go over in the morning and take Taylor out for breakfast, try to explain Kara's reasoning to him and make him see how much she loved him.

Finally exhausted, he lay down on the sofa and Mel curled up on the floor beside him. It was barely light when the telephone woke him up again. He was going to have to disconnect the damn thing, he thought as he stumbled to answer it.

He recognized Kara's voice but didn't understand a thing she said. She was crying.

"Kara, I'm not understanding you. Is it Taylor?"

The word "Gone!" came through clearly.

Still dressed from the night before, he grabbed his keys, called Mel to him and ran out to his truck.

Looking like death in his old gray sweats, her face pale, her hair in a disheveled ponytail, Kara showed Cole Taylor's empty room. "His backpack's gone, and he took all the money out of his truck bank. Cole, he's run away!"

"Okay, but he's still a little kid. He can't have gotten too far. How long's he been gone?"

"I'm not sure. I slept in the living room. I checked him about four a.m. and he was still there. I woke up about an hour later to the sound of wind on the roof…."

Cole remembered Taylor had said something about climbing onto the roof from his bedroom window to help put up the reindeer. The little boy could use the same technique to reach the plum tree and climb down to the ground.

The same thought must have occurred to Kara. She put both hands over her mouth and cried, "He climbed out his window!"

Cole held her briefly, then put her to work. "Find me something he wore yesterday or something he slept in, to give Mel his scent. I'm going to call the department."

That done, he called his aunt Shirley and asked her to come and sit with Kara.

"Do you have any thoughts on where he might have gone?" he asked as she followed him out to his truck.

"I've been racking my brain," she said miserably. "I can't think of anything. He's just so mad at me, he wanted to get away. He could be anywhere. Find him, Cole," she pleaded.

"I will," he promised as he locked Mel in the passenger seat. "Go inside and have a cup of coffee and something to eat. You have to keep your wits about you."

"If I had any wits, I'd have told him the truth in the first place!"

"Come on. No self-flagellation. That isn't going to help. I'll keep in touch. You call my cell if you hear anything."

Kara nodded, tears streaming down her face. She made a pathetic figure as she waved him off. He was relieved to see his aunt hurrying down the street on her way to stay with Kara. He tapped the horn lightly as he passed Shirley, and she blew him a kiss.

Cole did his best to suppress panic. He forced himself not to think about the things that could happen to a little kid walking alone at this hour. The sky was lightening to a cold gray as he drove slowly past the school, then did a quick walk through the playground with Mel, on the chance Taylor had recognized his truck and was hiding from him.

Then Cole cruised through the neighborhood, carefully checking both sides of the street, looking up side streets, watching for some sign of the familiar blue jacket. Nothing. How far could Taylor have gone?

In the shopping district nearby, early morning patrons wandered in and out of the bakery, the variety store, a coffee bar. Cole parked the truck and checked out each place, but no one had seen a boy wandering on his own.

He drove a little way down the highway, then turned around, certain Taylor couldn't have gone that far unless...someone had picked him up.

He didn't want to consider that, though he knew the department would be working on such a possibility.

This time he headed in the opposite direction and tried to reason where an eight-year-old would have gone. His first thought was a friend's house, but the mother would have called Kara by now.

Frustration was driving up his blood pressure and reducing his ability to think clearly. Mel whined in sympathy.

As Cole pulled out to pass a large tractor-trailer rig with a full load, a light suddenly went on in his brain.

Trucks! Taylor loved trucks! Cole remembered the night Kara and Taylor had helped him buy his Christmas tree and Cole had taken them to dinner. They'd passed the Esmee Engines plant not far from their neighborhood, and Taylor had talked about wanting to drive a big rig when he grew up. They'd speculated on where the trucks went, where the drivers stayed, what the best truck stops were. The plant was close enough that Taylor could have walked there.

"That's it, Mel!" Cole said, racing in the direction of the plant. Mel barked, catching Cole's excitement. Five minutes later Cole pulled onto the large concrete pad where Esmee Engines' fleet of trucks was usually parked. But only one truck was left there. Mel whined, eager to get to work.

Cole put the lead on him, gave him a good whiff of Taylor's pajamas and followed as the dog sniffed the air and then the ground, ignoring a man in coveralls who walked out of a loading bay and came toward them.

"Can I help you?" The man looked annoyed at their intrusion, even suspicious.

Cole remembered belatedly that he wasn't wearing a uniform or driving a department vehicle.

Restraining Mel, Cole pulled out his badge with his free hand. "I'm Officer Winslow with the Courage Bay P.D. We're looking for a missing boy about eight years old. He's fascinated by your trucks, and I thought he might be around here."

The man's manner became more receptive, though he shook his head. "Haven't seen a boy around."

Another man in jeans and a blue-and-gray flannel jacket walked out of the bay.

"Maldonado," the first man called to him. "You see a little boy around here this morning? This officer's looking for a lost kid."

Maldonado nodded, tucking the paper he held into

a pocket of his jacket. "'Bout an hour ago," he said. "I got a call on my cell phone, and by the time I hung up, he was gone. I figured he went home."

"Blue coat? Backpack? About eight years old?"

Maldonado frowned. "Big for eight. I'd have given him eleven or twelve—old enough to be on his own."

That was Taylor. "So, you didn't see him leave?"

Maldonado shook his head.

"Could he have gone inside the building?" Cole asked the other man, hope rising in him.

He shook his head. "I'd have seen him."

"Was the truck open?"

Maldonado nodded. "Steiner was loading up."

Mel barked furiously.

"Where's the truck going?" Cole asked, running Mel back to his own truck.

The other two men kept up with him. "His first stop's California Automotive. It's at the end of the Fortune Mall. You know, that little strip mall near the road to the freeway?"

"How long ago did he leave?"

"Not sure. Ten minutes?"

"Okay!" Cole ran around to the driver's side. "If I miss him, I'll call you for the rest of his schedule. Meanwhile, can you call him and warn him he might have a child in the semitrailer?"

The man shrugged apologetically. "Radio's not working in that rig. I'm sorry. We keep meaning to replace it..."

Cole shook his head. "What's the next stop after the strip mall?"

"About thirty miles away."

That wasn't good.

Maldonado handed him a business card. "There's the number of the plant. Anything else we can do?"

"I'll call if there is. Thanks."

He jumped into the truck and sped away, praying they were right about this, that Taylor was in the back of the rig and that he was safe. He called the station to tell them where he was going.

Cole made it to the Fortune Mall in seven minutes and saw with great relief that the big Esmee Engines truck was parked there, in front of California Automotive. A large Santa had been painted on the side of the container, his bag displaying the Esmee logo.

The back of the trailer was open, the loading ramp down. The driver was probably inside the store, making his deliveries. Cole said a little prayer that Taylor hadn't jumped out and taken off.

He gave Mel the scent again and let him loose. Barking excitedly, Mel ran to the truck and right up the ramp.

Taylor was inside.

Cole raced up the ramp himself. Boxes were piled high on either side, with only a small aisle down the middle for the driver.

"Taylor!" Cole shouted, making his way to the back.

He heard nothing but Mel's barking.

"Mel, stop!" Cole said firmly. In the silence he heard the dog's thumping tail. Mel had found Taylor.

"Taylor, it's Cole," he said, sidling back. "Come on out. You're not in trouble, I just want to take you home."

A pair of arms wrapped suddenly around his waist as boy and backpack slammed against him.

Cole hugged Taylor to him, grateful the boy was in one piece.

"I wanted to run away," Taylor said tearfully, "but I didn't know where to go! So I climbed into the truck. I was going to get out, but the door was locked and we were driving away and I knew I was in big trouble!"

"Come on." Cole took Taylor firmly by the hand and led him out of the dark trailer. At the ramp, he leaped down, reached up for Taylor and lifted the boy into his arms, holding on to him for a minute as Taylor sobbed his fear and relief.

"It's going to be all right," Cole said firmly. "I know you're feeling really bad, but it's nothing we can't fix or learn to live with."

"Mom probably hates me!"

"Never. She was frantic when she discovered you were gone. We're going to call her right now."

Taylor tightened his grip on Cole. "My dad's a bad guy."

"I know. But that doesn't really affect you, even though it feels like it does." Cole started for the truck, the boy still in his arms. Mel trotted beside him, pleased with himself for a job well done.

There was a small coffee shop next to the automotive store that was just opening for business. When Cole glanced at it, he noticed the driver coming out of California Automotive with an empty dolly. He wondered whether he should take the time to fill the guy in, but decided to leave that to his co-workers. The sooner Cole got Taylor back to Kara, the better.

Suddenly a giant, reverberating *boom* split the air. The earth shook, and glass shattered, flying everywhere. People screamed as Cole hit the ground, Taylor still in his arms. He shielded the boy with his body, gathering Mel close, too, as debris rained down on them.

Once the shower stopped, Cole raised his head to see that the front of the coffee shop and automotive store had been blown away. The awnings hung in tatters, all the windows were missing, and automotive parts were strewn over the parking lot.

Cole got to his feet, pulling Taylor up with him. "You okay?" he demanded.

Trembling, Taylor nodded.

Mel was already on duty, rooting through a pile of rubble in front of the coffee shop.

Taylor pointed his finger at the truck he'd been hiding in. "Look!" he said in a strangled whisper.

The entire back of the trailer was blown off, and the sides were turned and twisted. The remaining boxes of automotive parts sat burning on the concrete. Cole's heart lodged in his throat as he realized that only a minute ago, he and Taylor and Mel had been in that truck.

"Okay!" Galvanized into action, he turned to his own truck, saw mercifully that it remained in one piece, and hurried to put Taylor in it. He handed the boy his cell phone. "Call 911 for me," he said, "and tell them there's been an explosion at the Fortune Mall. Got that?"

"Yeah."

"Then call your mom and tell her you're all right, but that we might be a little while."

"Okay."

Cole ran over to Mel, who stood in front of the coffee shop, barking for him. He dreaded what he would find, remembering the two young women he'd seen walking toward the shop just before the explosion. But he was happily surprised to see one of them, bruised and dusty, tending to her friend, who was pinned on the ground by one of the awning poles. At least both women seemed alert.

Cole lifted the pole off the young woman.

"Jeez!" she said as Cole helped her to her feet. "Who needs a wake-up cup of coffee?"

A sense of humor was always a good sign, Cole figured. She brushed herself off, and she and her friend began looking around for their purses.

Cole directed them toward the far end of the parking lot. "Save the search until the fire trucks arrive, okay?"

Mel was already in the shop and barking furiously.

Behind the counter, a dazed young man stared at the gaping hole where the front wall had been.

Cole caught his arm and drew him out of the building. "Anyone else inside?" he asked. He had to repeat the question.

"Uh...no," the young man replied, finally coming around. "I work the first hour alone."

"Good. Please stay away from the shop. Police and fire department are on the way."

Mel had moved on to the automotive shop. The Esmee driver had a gash on his forearm, but he was well enough to help an older man in coveralls whose head was covered in blood. The driver put his handkerchief to the wound to stanch the flow.

"You two all right?" Cole asked.

The old guy nodded. "Yeah. I was in the back. I got down in time, but the cash register fell on my head." He smiled weakly. "Good thing there's never much money in it."

"Was there anyone else inside?" he asked, noticing Mel was sniffing the ground.

"No. I came in early to meet the delivery truck."

"What the hell happened?" the driver asked Cole.

Cole pointed to the back of his semitrailer. "Looks like something you were carrying exploded. You two sit tight. There's an ambulance on its way." Cole called Mel to him and checked the rest of the mall for damage. A crowd of people had started to gather, some to see if they could help, others just to gawk.

The emergency services units arrived with a couple of fire trucks and several ambulances. Everyone was relieved to see how minimal the injuries and damage were, considering how mangled the truck was.

Cole intercepted Dan Egan, the fire chief. He was a big guy, in his forties and well-respected. Cole told him what he'd seen.

Dan nodded, then walked with Cole to the damaged truck. "Looks like a job for Sam," he said.

Sam Prophet was the fire department's arson investigator.

The fire chief frowned at Cole. "This is the same truck where you found the missing kid?"

"Yeah." There was a hitch in Cole's breath, and in the beat of his heart. "I'd just gotten him out, and we were walking across the parking lot to my truck with Mel when it blew."

Dan clapped him on the back. "You got your Christmas gift a couple of days early."

Cole knew that. It was another miracle.

After checking in with the police officer in charge, Cole left to take Taylor home.

A fire truck was positioned between him and his vehicle. When he ran around it, Mel following, he found Kara leaning into the cab of his truck, Taylor wrapped in her arms. She was squeezing the life out of him while he tried to assure her in a strangled voice that he was fine. Shirley stood beside them, dabbing at her eyes with a tissue.

"Me and Cole and Mel were walking across the parking lot and there was this *boom*!" Taylor flung both arms wide open, forcing Kara to release him. "All this burning stuff fell on Cole, but he was laying on me and Mel, so we didn't get hurt."

"Burning stuff...!" Cole heard her gasp. "Where *is* Cole?"

"I'm right here," Cole said, thinking how selfish it was of him to be pleased at how worried she looked. "I'm fine," he reassured her.

"Oh, Cole!" She hugged him with surprising strength. "When Taylor called and told me what happened, I couldn't just sit home and wait, so Shirley drove us here. Is Mel okay?"

Mel barked at the sound of his name and licked her hand.

Shirley reached around Kara to pat Cole's shoulder. "I know you'd have rather she waited, but she was determined."

Kara pushed him away and turned him around. "There's a giant hole in your shirt!" she exclaimed.

He was surprised to feel her fingertips on his bare back.

"Well, you're burned, but I don't think it's too bad. I'll put some stuff on it when we get home." She turned him around again. "Can you leave?"

"Yeah. We got lucky. No serious injuries, and the fires will be out in no time. Want to come to my house so I can get another shirt?"

He'd been so busy savoring the love in Kara's eyes that he hadn't noticed that Taylor had both arms around his waist and was squeezing him tightly.

Kara's gaze went to her son, then to Cole. She looked surprised.

Cole put a hand on Taylor's back. "And I have an angel that should be installed on top of the tree. Christmas is only four days away."

"Yeah." Taylor's reply was calmly contented rather than wildly excited. "Can I ride home with you?" he asked Cole.

"I'll just go on my way," Shirley said, "so the three of you can..."

"I need to talk to Cole alone," Taylor said seriously. "Is that okay, Aunt Shirley? Can you take Mom to Cole's house?"

"If you call me *your* aunt Shirley," she said with a beaming smile, "I'll do anything you want." She caught Kara's arm and drew her along with her to her car.

Kara looked at Cole and her son over her shoulder as she was led away, apparently not sure whether she should be worried.

Cole felt the same way. He put Mel in the back, making a mental note to give him a steak when they got home because of his on-his-toes performance this morning, then closed Taylor into the passenger seat and climbed in behind the wheel.

He maneuvered carefully around various emergency vehicles before finally turning onto the road, which was clogged with onlookers. It was a few minutes before he got by them and headed for home.

Taylor, deciding the time was right, turned toward Cole and said gravely, "You know I have a father."

"I do," Cole replied. "And I know he's in jail, and you're mad at me because I didn't tell you. I'm sorry about that."

"That's okay. I was thinking about it in the back of the truck. Mom just wanted me to think he was good. And you love Mom, so you like to do what she wants."

That summed it up pretty well.

"Anyway, that's not what I want to talk about. I mean, not exactly."

"Okay. What do you want to talk about?"

He fidgeted a little, opened his mouth to speak, then closed it again. Cole glanced at him worriedly and saw that the usually plainspoken boy appeared to be embarrassed.

"Just say what you're thinking," he encouraged. "It's okay to be honest. You're not going to hurt my feelings, or make me angry."

Taylor's embarrassment turned to confusion. "I was going to talk about me."

"Oh." Prepared to go wherever this conversation was taking them, Cole nodded, grateful for the straight stretch of road and the quiet traffic that allowed him to split his concentration. "Okay. Go ahead."

"Okay." Taylor leaned slightly toward him. "I'm pretty good in school. I'm not very good at sports, but

I like to watch football and baseball. I usually do what I'm told, but sometimes I forget." He sighed, then admitted candidly, "Well, I don't really forget. Sometimes I just want to do what I want to do, and Mom's scared of everything. And when you're bigger than all the other kids, you have to act like you're older—and braver. I have a couple of stitches in my head from riding a bike on a split-rail fence. But I won't do that again. I bled all over the place and Mom really freaked."

It took Cole a minute to realize Taylor was selling himself. He pulled off the road and stopped the truck.

Unbuckling his seat belt, he put a hand to Taylor's dusty, disheveled hair. "I'm already convinced you're pretty special, Taylor. What are you trying to tell me?"

Taylor swallowed, his eyes huge and uncertain. "I was just wondering...would you like to have a kid like me?"

Cole felt an old wound close and an entire future open up.

"I'd like that a lot," he replied finally. "And I know you're worried about what your dad would think...."

Taylor shook his head, his expression alarmingly mature. "No. Not anymore. I don't think he really loves me." He smiled cautiously at Cole. "But you do, don't you?"

"Big-time." Cole unfastened Taylor's seat belt and took him into his arms.

Taylor hugged him tightly. "Then maybe we should have Christmas after all."

TWENTY MINUTES LATER Cole stood Taylor halfway up the ladder he'd placed near the tree. Cole held onto the boy, who was leaning over to place the angel tree-topper with her Love banner on the topmost branch of the magical tree.

Kara, Shirley, and Brad and Emily applauded. Mel barked and wagged his tail. Kara had called Brad to assess the burn on Cole's back. He'd brought Emily and Little Brad with him, and quickly determined that it was a first-degree burn and barely worthy of sympathy. But he'd washed it carefully, put antibacterial cream on it and covered it with a wide bandage from the medical bag he kept in the car.

Cole swung Taylor to the floor again. Kara's heart was so full, she couldn't speak. Something had happened between her son and Cole on their way home from the strip mall where she'd almost lost both of them. Neither of them had volunteered to share the content of their conversation, and she wouldn't ask. But she could see that whatever they'd discussed had lightened her son's emotional burden considerably and given him a new confidence with Cole.

She said a silent prayer of thanks for getting everything she'd wanted for Christmas.

"Why don't you all stay for lunch?" she asked Cole's family. "If I can't find anything in the cupboard, we'll order something."

"Sounds good to me." Brad pointed to a burned-out bulb on the tree. "While you're doing that, I'll see if I can fix the bad bulb. Taylor, you helped put this up. You know where the extra bulbs are?"

Emily excused herself to feed the baby, and Shirley ran home to bring back cookies for dessert.

Alone in the kitchen with Cole, Kara wrapped her arms around him and kissed him thoroughly, so grateful to have him safe and sound—and in her life.

"Do you have any idea how much I love you?"

"Just barely," he said, his eyes smoky with desire. "You'll have to keep telling me over and over."

She kissed him again, long and lingeringly. And then she became aware that they weren't alone. She raised her head to see Taylor watching them, his eyes alight with happiness.

"Isn't there a corny old song about a kid seeing his mom kissing Santa Claus?" he teased.

Kara laughed, still holding on to Cole. "There is. Do you know what it means?"

"Yeah," he said, beaming. "Santa Claus is the kid's dad."

Ordinary people. Extraordinary circumstances.
Meet a new generation of heroes—
the men and women of
Courage Bay Emergency Services.
CODE RED
A new Harlequin continuity series continues
January 2005 with

NIGHTWATCH
by Jo Leigh

E.R. chief Dr. Guy Giroux is shocked. His ex-wife's eighteen-year-old daughter died during childbirth—in *his* E.R. He didn't even know she was pregnant. Guy confronts Dr. Rachel Browne, demanding answers. Rachel could be stubborn, obstinate and downright hardheaded—but faced with Guy's grief and anger she's disarmingly calm, compassionate…even tender. And as Guy and Rachel hunt down the truth, Guy realizes how much he wants to keep the baby…and how much he wants Rachel, too.

Here's a preview!

Guy sighed. "I heard from Walter. Heather's father."

"Oh?" Rachel asked.

"Bastard can't make it here until next week. Says he's in the middle of a business deal. Wanted to know about the funeral."

"What did you tell him?"

"That I'm waiting for Tammy. It's her decision."

"Is that all?"

Leaning back in his chair, Guy stared up at the wall behind her. He looked tired, defeated. And so sad.

"I gave him a few choice thoughts. Useless, of course."

"So forget about him. Tell me what's going on with Heath."

"He's stabilized. But it's not great. He's probably going to need an operation on his heart, but right now it's his kidney function that's paramount.... You know the drill. I'm just grateful at this point that he's hanging on."

Rachel looked down at her hands, at the manicure

she'd had yesterday. The blatant honesty coming from Guy made her think of five excuses to leave. She wasn't used to this casual frankness from him. It disarmed her and made her feel vulnerable. But she'd keep going, testing this new ground. She raised her gaze and took a deep breath.

"It has to be very hard for you."

"It is. I never had a child of my own, but this..." He leaned forward, his eyes moist. "Nothing can happen to him, Rachel."

"He's getting the best care possible."

"I know. But I can't—" His voice broke.

She stood up, went to his side and crouched down next to him, touching his arm gently. "You can't be the one. I know. You're used to being the doctor. The one who pulls the rabbit out of the hat. The person who saves lives against all odds. The people looking after Heath are the very best in the field, Guy, and they're going to move heaven and earth to save him. All you can do now is love him."

Guy opened his mouth, but nothing came out. No words at all, and yet she understood his anguish, his frustration. Perhaps it was only something doctors could feel, when all their education, all their training meant nothing.

But there was something more, something that made her pulse quicken in fear. His look wasn't that of a man in pain, but of a man in need. A man who needed her. It was as if he was calling out to her, screaming to her to save him.

"Oh God, Guy. I can't—"

He leaned toward her and put his hand on hers. "Rachel."

His gaze raked her face, and the intensity of his expression took her breath. It was as if he could see inside her. Deep into her secrets.

And then he moved closer still, close enough that she felt his warm breath caress her cheek and she could see the flecks of gold in the depths of his eyes.

His lips touched hers, so gently, and she closed her eyes, trying not to bolt. She wanted to let herself feel—the texture of his lips, the tenderness, the way his hand squeezed hers so tightly. His need for her was in his touch, in his breath.

When he rose, he brought her up with him, his kiss deepening as his hand left hers and slipped to the back of her neck. He pulled her against him, and she was swamped by the physical sensations swirling inside her.

Her hands moved up his back, and for this moment, she was with him, trying to give him comfort. She'd never wanted to be so much to one person. Healing this way was completely foreign to her.

"Oh, that's just great."

Rachel jumped back at the intrusive voice, her face burning and every part of her shutting down. She didn't recognize the woman standing just inside Guy's office.

Guy sighed. "Tammy."

"You can't even wait till she's buried?" His ex-wife

walked inside, her fury making her seem much taller than her diminutive frame.

Blond, beautiful, dressed in tight black leather pants and a red, low-cut sweater, she looked like the perfect trophy wife. Her makeup was flawless and not a hair was out of place, but her fury was palpable as her gaze moved from Guy to Rachel and back.

"You have to do your whore right here, in your office? In the same hospital where that baby lies dying?"

Annette Broadrick
Stella Bagwell
Kathie DeNosky
You never know what surprises your holiday getaway will bring...
Getaway

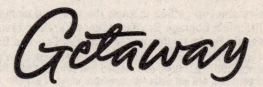

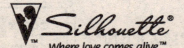

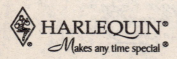

A sizzling new longer-length story in Secrets!, the bestselling Silhouette Desire® miniseries from…

National bestselling author

BARBARA McCAULEY

BLACKHAWK LEGACY

Dillon Blackhawk
had run as fast and far from
his past as he could…now
Rebecca Blake was asking
him to confront it.

"Ms. McCauley makes your eyes race across each page as you revel in absolutely sizzling romance."
—*Romantic Times* on BLACKHAWK'S SWEET REVENGE

Available in December 2004.

Visit Silhouette Books at www.eHarlequin.com

PSBL

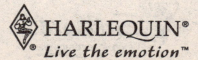

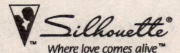

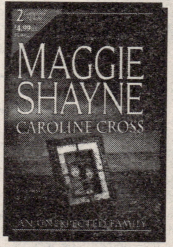

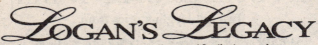

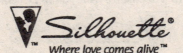